On the Cutting Edge
Retribution

By J.J. Luepke
© 2012

Order this book online at www.trafford.com
or email orders@trafford.com

Most Trafford titles are also available at major online book retailers.

Printed in the United States of America.

ISBN: 978-1-4669-6078-7 (sc)
ISBN: 978-1-4669-6077-0 (e)

Library of Congress Control Number: 2012918269

Trafford rev. 10/15/2012

 www.trafford.com

North America & international
toll-free: 1 888 232 4444 (USA & Canada)
phone: 250 383 6864 ♦ fax: 812 355 4082

Dedication

This book is dedicated to my hometown editing team of R. Kramer, Advertising Agent and SAM, Lakeview Writers Club Facilitator. These two make the perfect cleanup team; Kramer cleans up my typos, and SAM keeps my story line running clearly and smoothly. Thank you ladies from the bottom of my very grateful heart!

—J.J. Luepke

Chapter One

Memories

"Mayor Glass! To what do I owe the honor of your visit?" Eleanor Buchannon held the hand carved wooden door of her home open for the city official to enter. The robust man, in a gray suit and ponytail, removed his hat and strode into the foyer. His walking stick clattered on the doorframe as he twirled to face her.

"Mrs. Buchannon, Eleanor, if I may," he said with an overabundance of warmth. "That's a lovely lavender outfit you're wearing, much like the choir gowns from high school. If you recall, we were in the choir together back then."

"Thank you for the compliment. Yes, sir, I believe I do remember that. You were the baritone and couldn't decide whether to sing bass or second tenor." They both chuckled.

"Indeed, that was so. I have made many more important decisions since then. In fact, last week I purchased your neighbor's house to the right. I would very much like to make an offer on your home as well. Surely, with your granddaughter getting married, she will be moving away; and, you will be left with all that yard work and snow removal. Certainly, a woman of your stature shouldn't be doing all that manual labor."

"Should I choose not to do it myself, Mayor, I could always hire it done."

"True, true; however, why should you make that kind of expenditure when you have a willing buyer right in front of you? I would be more than generous in my offer, which would allow you to retire in style—perhaps obtain a quaint little condominium across town if you wish to continue to own your own place; or, perhaps rent a small apartment on Main Street where you don't have to drive to the grocery store? One with an elevator so you wouldn't have to climb stairs. Wouldn't that be convenient?"

"I thank you for your concern, Mayor; but, I haven't given it a thought just yet. But, I'm certain that I won't have to make that decision today."

"Please call me 'Ellis'. 'Mayor' is just too formal, especially if we're going to be doing business together. Besides, aren't you in Ladies Aid with Joanie? I would certainly want to treat my wife's friends with a great deal of care. In fact, I would be willing to pay you full market value for your home. I'm sure a nice young family would be interested in renting it."

"As I said, Mayor Glass," Eleanor said as she opened the front door, indicating it was time for him to leave. "I haven't thought much about selling my house just yet. I will let you know should I decide to sell it to you."

"Just think what a lovely bed and breakfast it would make," the mayor kept at her. "Wouldn't that be a nice addition to our lovely town?" The mayor was fierce today. "I can just picture the Christmas tree in your tower window and lights strung around the entry to every room in this spacious Victorian Lady. Or, perhaps, a young couple with a growing family may need a place to rent while they get established financially . . ."

"Be that as it may, the answer is still 'No'."

"Mark my words, Eleanor; no one in town will offer you as much as I have for this old house. Please remember everything I've said and give me a call at the City office when you decide to sell." He slammed his hat onto his head and scowled like a bulldog as he stomped toward the door of the Buchannon home, then turned as if to try one last time to convince her to sell.

"No, Mr. Mayor," Eleanor Buchannon said sternly. "I repeat: My home is not for sale at this time, not at any price. If you have no further topics of discussion today, sir, I bid you adieu!"

"We shall see about that, Eleanor!" the mayor replied as he snapped his cane and headed out the door. His ponytail was incongruent with the business suit he was wearing. "I have quoted you a top-dollar offer. Call me if you change your mind."

Eleanor was right on his heels as he exited the charming Victorian home in which she and her granddaughter, Josie, lived in Lakewood, New York. She slammed the door behind her and turned in a huff. *Grrr! That man has gotten under my skin ever since he tried to kiss me in high school*, she thought as she yanked on the hem of her vest in irritation. She marched to the kitchen. A hot cup of chamomile tea would help calm her jangled nerves. She put the kettle on, set out a clean cup and rummaged through the tea cabinet for the right box. When the kettle was on, Eleanor went to the telephone to call her granddaughter. Josie should know about this immediately!

< * >

"Good morning, boss!" Vikki Dale bubbled with joy at seeing her employer and best friend enter the door of

Sanderson & Sons Advertising Agency Monday morning. "Did you have a great weekend?"

"It was phenomenal!" Josie Buchannon said. "Helping P.J. move into his own apartment right here in Lakewood is like a dream come true! I'm so glad he got that job at Lakewood Technologies last month. He's been living with a co-worker, and commuting to his parent's on the weekends. This way we will be able to see more of each other, and actually get to date!"

"I can't imagine you had much opportunity with him living in New York City, even if it was only 90 miles away. Besides, you were kind of busy with the FBI investigation for a while."

Josie didn't want to remember the events that took place only a couple of months ago, but no one in town seemed to want to let her. They were always complimenting her on her courage, bravery and guts. It was redundant, all the way around. The newspaper had printed a banner story on how she helped the FBI catch her attacker and murderer of their employer, Lewis Sanderson. Josie had been run out of town at knifepoint and had to find a different job in New York City. This left her grandmother vulnerable, but she had been assured the police would patrol her street more frequently than usual. Then Mr. Sanderson was murdered, with Viagra® of all things! On the heels of this news, the FBI showed up at Garvey, Sloan and Associates, LTD, where Josie was, by then, making her way, and asked her to come back to Lakewood to help catch the killer. Being a target wasn't something Josie relished, but she enjoyed putting together her "Princess Plan" to accomplish the task. The name seemed appropriate at the time because Mr. Sanderson's lawyer had also arrived in the Big Apple to announce that Mr. Sanderson had been Josie's illegitimate father and that he had left his massive estate to her. Because of that creative plan, the office was now fortified with security cameras, intercom, and sturdier locks on the doors.

With Josie pulling strings anonymously through the estate lawyer, Vikki had been hired to replace Donna Schmidt at the front desk when Donna was transferred to production to assist Hilda Shoemaker. The staff also included Jessica Springer who was the agency's ad model and research assistant. When Josie made her debut as the new owner of Sanderson & Sons, she created quite an irritation for suspected killer Cassandra Coven, the agency's manager. Josie set up scenarios in which Cass's own scathing comments were thrown back at her and her internet access was blocked. Josie was also able to prove that Cass didn't have much creativity and had stolen a lot of Josie's ideas in the past. This was all done purposely and was carefully monitored by the FBI to catch Cass when she finally cracked. She came in one night when Josie was supposedly working late and confronted Josie with a gun. Luckily, Josie's fiancé, P.J. Coleson arrived on the scene in time to knock Cass off her aim, because Cass had locked the basement door, preventing the undercover FBI agent from getting there in time.

Josie shivered at the memory of the near miss. "Let's not bring that up again. I would much rather look forward to planning my wedding and talking about bridesmaid dresses with my maid of honor over lunch today. What do you say? My treat!"

"Certainly!" Vikki said. "I can't wait to show you the dress I found in this month's issue of Bride's Magazine®!"

"Great! Now back to work! Any messages for me?"

"There are a couple: Your nine o'clock said she wanted to come in a thirty minutes early as she had another meeting to get to at noon, and it requires some driving. And, your grandmother called. She wants you to be sure to call her at your earliest convenience. She has a meeting and won't be home for supper. She has something important to discuss with you."

"Whew! I guess I'd better get ready for my eight-thirty meeting, then," Josie said. "See you later!" With that, she marched on through the swinging doors to the main advertising room. Greeting the rest of the staff on her way through, she continued to the back where her office was located. She pulled the keys out of her coat pocket and unlocked the door. She was reaching for the light switch when Nathan Danielson came out of his office.

"Good morning, Josie!" he said. "If you have a moment, sometime today, I would like to go over this month's accounting figures with you."

"Good morning to you, too! Yes, I believe I have some time early this afternoon. I should be back from lunch shortly after one. How about then?"

"Thanks!" Nathan said, then spun around and returned to his office. Josie proceeded into her own office and set her briefcase on the desk. Walking around it, she booted up her computer and brought up her schedule. She adjusted it to accommodate the change in her first appointment, and went to the file cabinet to pull the files on First Federal Bank. She would be meeting with their vice president of public relations, Patricia Vizecky in just under an hour. Josie also opened her laptop computer on which she had stored a couple of prospective ads for the back, which she had drawn up at home the night before. She plugged it into the computer and made a couple of last minute adjustments before printing out two copies. When she was satisfied she was ready for the meeting, she grabbed her purse and flitted across the hall to the bathroom to freshen her lipstick. In one of the many magazine ads she had studied over the past couple of years, Josie was aware of how much more seriously people took women when they wore lipstick. Something about it polished off the professional look. After primping, Josie returned to her office to call her grandmother and check her email while she waited.

"Hey, Grams! Vikki said you have a meeting tonight," Josie said when her grandmother picked up. "That's your ladies aid meeting at church, right?"

"Yes, dear, it is. The other thing I wanted to tell you about is that Mayor Glass stopped by today and made an offer on the house. He wasn't pleased when I turned him down. I just wanted you to know about that."

"Thanks for including me," Josie said. "I will pray he accepts your answer. I know how determined he can be to get what he wants. I have to go now, Grams. I am expecting a client any minute now."

"I thought you said your first appointment wasn't until nine o'clock," Grams said, "but, I know how things can change, so I will say goodbye. Love you, Josie Girl."

"Love you too, Grams! Bye!"

Vikki's voice came over the intercom announcing that Ms. Vizecky had arrived.

"Thank you, Vikki. Please ask if she would like a cup of coffee, or water; and, then bring her back." In just a minute, Vikki was tapping lightly on Josie's open door and escorting Ms. Vizecky into the office.

"Good morning, Pat!" Josie stood and extended her hand. Pat shook it. "Have a seat on the couch."

"Thank you." Pat accepted the invitation. "It's already eighty degrees outside. It's going to be a warm September, the way it's starting out."

"Yes. Thank God for central air!" Josie sat in her chair and picked up her printouts. "When you called last week to make this appointment, I was glad you gave me some pointers as to what you had in mind. I took the liberty of putting these sketches together over the weekend. Tell me what you think about them."

The other woman took the offering and paged through them, nodding as she did so.

"Of course, we would replace the photos with actual pictures of your employees in the appropriate roles," Josie said. She grasped the edge of her chair to release some nervous energy, hoping Pat didn't notice. She smiled as Pat looked up.

"These look good," Pat said. "I was hoping you would offer to photograph my staff. They deserve recognition. Since this is the 50th anniversary of the bank, we also want to recognize that. In fact, since you have done television commercials in the past, I was wondering if you couldn't turn this into a made for TV ad, as well as a printed one."

"Yes! I am sure Hildy can do that for you. Were there any other changes you would like to make? Have you redesigned your logo recently, or is that something you might consider? This would be a good time to show both the old and introduce the new one. I have taken the liberty of creating a couple of suggestions for that." Josie picked up another set of designs from the briefcase file and handed them to Pat.

"That is an interesting proposition," Pat said. "I will look them over and discuss them with the bank president. May I take these with me?"

"Yes, of course. Here's a file folder to carry them in." Josie handed her the manila folder she brought them in. "If you want the ads to start running next week, I would need your decision by this Thursday," Josie said.

"Understood," Pat said, offering her hand. "Thank you for the fine work you have already done on the bank's behalf. I will be in touch." Josie shook her hand and walked her to the door.

The intercom buzzed. "P.J. is on line one."

"Thanks, Vikki!" Josie returned to her desk and sat down to take the call. "Hello, P.J.! You don't usually call me at work. What's up?"

"I am at the hospital," he said. "There was an accident at work."

Chapter Two
P.J.'s Problems

"P.J., what happened?" Josie asked as she rushed into the emergency room at Lakewood General Hospital ten minutes later. She took one look at him and nearly fainted. His left eye was black and blue and his right hand was heavily bandaged.

"I'm not sure. One minute everything was fine. The next, my equipment blew up, right beneath my hands. The handle flew into my eye, and my hand slid onto the jagged edge of the lever." He waved the bandaged appendage for emphasis. The boss said I must have let my pen fall into the equipment or some other object. It threw the mechanism off, and when I tried to reverse the action by jerking on the lever, the lever broke."

"Gosh, honey! I'm glad you weren't killed!"

"Me, too, obviously," P.J. said with a lopsided grin. Then the grin faded away. "The only thing is, as you know, I don't drink pop, and my pen was in my work boot the whole time!" He lifted his right leg and twisted it inward. With his left hand, he hitched up his pant leg to reveal the writing instrument hanging on the inside next to his ankle. He looked up with raised eyebrows.

"What's the company going to do about it?" Josie asked. She stepped closer to the examination table and patted her fiancé on the shoulder.

"They said they are going to pull the machine apart to see what caused it. When they find it, they will turn it over to the police for finger printing. A fat lot of good that will do, most of the guys wear gloves." P.J. snorted.

Just then a nurse came in with P.J.'s pain reliever and walking papers. She looked Josie in the eye and said, "Don't let him drive under the influence of this medication." Turning to P.J., she said, "You, young man, are not to go back to work until you come back for a follow-up appointment. Your hand is fractured. Let's put on this wrist brace. Leave it on except to ice your hand a couple of times tonight and three times tomorrow. Do not use your hand until it has been X-rayed again."

"Yes, Ma'am!" P.J. barked in response. Josie had to turn away to hide a snicker.

After the nurse left the room, Josie tried to help P.J. ease himself off the exam table and out the door to the waiting car. On the trip back to P.J.'s apartment, he shared a couple of other work-related incidents that took place since he started at Lakewood Technologies.

It seems there has been a rash of petty little accidents in and around P.J.'s workstation that couldn't quite be explained: Office supplies missing, his office chair lost a wheel, and, the funniest of all was the name plaques on the rest rooms had been switched. P.J. had walked into the ladies' room on his first day at work. Luckily, the only occupant had already finished using the toilet and was already washing her hands.

"If I didn't know any better," Josie said, "I would say you were being hazed, just like some college freshman!"

"My boss has started thinking that, too! After today's incident, he promised to get security cameras up to try to catch the culprit, or culprits. I don't know why they didn't have them up already. I thought every industry uses them. And, I said so. The shift manager agreed with me. In addition, management has transferred me out of Research and Development to Engineering. I'll be riding a desk for a while."

"I'm sorry to hear that. Hopefully, it's only temporary. Are you sure you don't want to come back to the house with me?" Josie asked as they mounted the stairs to his second story walk-up. "How are you going to take these pills if you can't use your hand?"

"Easy! I'll have you empty them into a bowl by the sink, and I can just pick one out with my left hand!" P.J. grinned at her, as he often did these days. It was like a special smile just for her. It melted her heart.

"Okay," was all she could manage. P.J. gave her his keys, and she unlocked the apartment door. She led him over to the couch where he plunked down a little too hard sending a jolt through his hand. He moaned at the pain.

"You. Be. Careful." She admonished. "You don't want that fracture to splinter some more!"

She went to the cupboard to fulfill his request regarding the prescription, and tried to lay out other items he would be needing to get along one-handed. "Have you had lunch? How about I fix you something to eat?"

"I'm not . . . really . . . hungry . . ." P.J. yawned and swiveled to lie down, pulling his feet onto the couch. He yawned again. "I think . . . the pain pills . . . are . . . kicking . . . in." He barely got the sentence out and he was asleep.

As Josie picked up the afghan from the nearby chair and draped it over him, she was reminded of the night they met. His mother had rented the apartment over their garage to

Josie instead of letting her stay at the YMCA in New York City. P.J. had come home from college earlier than expected, arriving in the middle of the night, and had planned to sneak into the apartment. It had been his bedroom his last year in high school. His banging on the door had startled her awake. They were both surprised to encounter each other in the middle of the night. Once the shock had worn off and the introductions made P.J. accepted her invitation to sleep on the couch rather than awaken anyone in the house. Josie had awakened before he did the next morning and watched him sleep, curled up in a fetal position. *I think I fell in love with him in that moment*, she thought, as she gazed fondly at him in the present.

Shaking her head to bring her mind to her chores, Josie decided to make P.J. a sandwich and leave it in the refrigerator, along with sliced peaches in a covered bowl that would be easy to open one-handed. Then she wrote a note saying she would stop by after work and make supper for him if the sandwich wasn't enough. She hated having to go back to work, but the meetings were starting to pile up. Josie picked up P.J.'s cellphone to make sure the battery was charged and set it back on the end table when she was satisfied it held enough juice to call her—or 911—if he needed help. Looking around, she couldn't see or think of anything else she could do at the moment, so she turned and left.

Everyone at the office was buzzing about P.J.'s accident, speculating on what happened and why. They nearly attacked Josie as she entered the door, asking how P.J. was. She gave all the information she had, with the exception of the possibility of hazing. She left that out.

"That's all I know for now. I can't imagine how it happened unless Lakewood Technologies uses faulty equipment."

"I know!" Jessica shouted. "Someone at work resents the fact that P.J. got a job there so quickly. I just bet his boss is noticing what a hard worker he is, and they can't stand it! They're sabotaging him! They're trying to make him look sloppy, careless and accident-prone!"

"Whatever is happening," Josie said, "I hope they get to the bottom of it soon—before anyone else gets hurt . . . or worse!"

Chapter Three
The Ladies Aid Angle

"You seem a bit shaken, Grams," Josie said after greeting her grandmother upon arriving at home after work. "Let me drive you to your ladies aid meeting tonight." She had taken one look at Eleanor and decided to wait until after the ladies aid meeting had had a reassuring affect on her grandmother before telling her about P.J.'s work accident.

"Only if you promise to stay for the meeting, pussycat." Eleanor stared her down. "We need more young blood like you to bring up more current topics than we sometimes digress to."

"You're right about that, Grams!" Josie snorted. "The ladies aid has a reputation of being a bunch of old biddies sitting around, drinking coffee, and planning their next bake sale!"

"Wait just a minute, Josie-girl! Those bake sales are legitimate fundraisers to help support our seminary students and missionaries. Besides, who doesn't like to eat baked goods at Christmas? Seems to me, you were one of biggest supporters last fall."

"So I was. However, I gave it all away as Christmas gifts at the office!"

"All the better! You were a selfless saint, and the seminary students loved you for it, I'm sure. Let me just collect my things and we can head out. I hope you don't mind grabbing drive-through supper tonight. As you can imagine, I don't feel like cooking after the run-in I had with the mayor."

"Then it's unfortunate that we'll probably be running into Mrs. Mayor at ladies aid!" Josie chuckled, hoping her grandmother wasn't too upset to appreciate a little humor. She was rewarded when her grandmother playfully slapped her shoulder and said, "Oh, you!"

Locking the house, the ladies left in Josie's new Chevy Impala and jovially argued over which of the two drive-through establishments they should patronize. Eleanor finally gave in as she knew the servers for ladies aid would be offering her favorite dessert tonight, and she didn't want to spoil her appetite before she got there with a heavy supper. It seemed to make sense that Josie would get what she wanted since she seldom ate dessert anyway.

They sat in the church parking lot for the few minutes it took them to finish the take-out. They exited the car brushing crumbs off their slacks. When they straightened up, they came face to face with Mrs. Ellis Glass. Josie wondered if her ears were burning. She quickly looked away while her grandmother took the opposite approach.

"Good evening, Joan," Eleanor said brightly. "How are you tonight?"

"Quite well, thank you, Eleanor! I hope you're well, too! And, I see you've brought a guest! How nice to see you again, Josephine! Thank you for coming to our ladies aid meeting!"

Josie was forced to look up with a smile. "Thank you, Mrs. Glass. But, please call me Josie—everyone does."

Mrs. Glass extended her free arm as a shepherd's hook and directed the Buchanon ladies toward the church as she continued. "As you know, tonight we will begin the new office selection process. Perhaps you two would be interested in holding office. I'm certain we could find a position for each of you . . . and, I would very much enjoy working with you!"

Josie wasn't as certain she would enjoy working with Mrs. Glass. The lady seemed to dominate the conversation and dole out compliments like the proverbial a used car salesman. *No offense to used-car salesmen,* Josie thought. That's just the first euphemism that popped into her head. *Gee, for an advertising agent, I have to get some udapted quip lines!* Josie held the side door open for the two older women and then followed them inside. They went single-file down the basement stairs. Except for the night's servers, they were the first to arrive.

Mrs. Glass went to the head table and opened her briefcase to withdraw the meeting agenda and a few other documents. Eleanor pointed to the ladies room, and Josie followed.

"Is she always like that? Sticky sweet?" Josie whispered.

"Mostly at election time," Eleanor said, also whispering.

When they had finished primping and returned to the common room, they noticed another half-dozen members had arrived. They greeted one another and found seating in the array of chairs facing the head table. Presently, Mrs. Glass was joined by secretary Joy Henderson and treasurer Nola Thompson. Mrs. Glass went over the agenda with them in hushed tones, occasionally looking up to check the growing crowd. Josie slumped in her seat as Mrs. Glass' eyes came to rest on her. Glancing away, she mumbled, "Not me! Don't you dare!"

"What, pussycat?" Grams asked. "Did you say something?"

"It's nothing. I just noticed Mrs. Glass looking this way. I don't want an office, Grams. I hope she knows that."

"Don't worry," Eleanor said, patting Josie's shoulder. "I think Mrs. Glass' friends will be filling each of the openings. That's usually how it works. The only exception would be if she were to be defeated by her opponent. In which case, she would revolve to the vice president seat. That is an automatic appointment because, having been president, she will easily be able to cover a meeting should the new president become ill, move away or for any other reason be unable to fulfill her duties."

"Heaven help the new president if she's someone other than Mrs. Glass!" Josie whispered.

"Amen!" She thought she heard her grandmother respond.

Another glance around the room showed the numbers had doubled as the clocked ticked its way toward the 7 o'clock starting time. St. Andrew's was a small parish so the 15 active members were the lot for this organization, and they were all out tonight due to elections.

Mrs. Glass called the meeting to order and asked the pastor's wife to give the devotion. Cindy Van Meveren stood with her devotion book at an angle between the group and the head table. She clearly gave a reading on how pride goes before a fall. Josie listened intently wondering if Cindy had intentionally picked this particular verse or if she had a little help. Or, maybe it was just a coincidence.

After the devotion, organist Erma Hawkinson led the attendees in the singing of *Amazing Grace*. It was her stand-by piece if she wasn't able to find out what the devotion topic was in order to coordinate. Josie was remembering all these little tell-tales Grams had shared with her after previous meetings. Eleanor would get a kick out of telling her granddaughter what happened, but then get remorseful, saying, "May God forgive me for gossiping!"

The reports and correspondence were dealt with in depth as Mrs. Glass was nothing if not thorough. Josie hid a yawn. It seemed like every bit of what was read in the minutes was then regurgitated during the Old Business section. Josie started wobbling back and forth, fighting passing out. Eleanor gave her a jab in the ribs. "Wake up!" it was meant to convey. Josie pasted a fake smile on her face and thought, *Well, I asked for this when I volunteered to drive Grams to the meeting.* She couldn't for the life of her figure out what her grandmother saw in belonging to a club like this.

Finally, Mrs. Glass asked for the nominations committee to give their report to start the election process.

Cindy Van Meveren stood up with a piece of notepaper twitching in her hand. She cleared her throat and looked around the room. She cleared her throat again before speaking.

"This is the slate of candidates which the nominations committee came up with—for Treasurer: Incumbant Nola Thompson will be opposed by Gina Vizecky, for Secretary, Incumbant Joy Henderson will be opposed by myself, Cindy Van Meveren . . .

A glance at Mrs. Glass told Josie the woman was getting anxious to get down to hearing her own name read and finding out who had the audacity to oppose her. The lady was barely sitting on the edge of her chair. She was fidgeting with her pen and biting her lip. Josie looked back at Cindy, whose forehead was now glistening with nervous perspiration as she continued . . .

"For preisdent, Incumbant Joan Glass is opposed by Eleanor Buchannon. The committee moves nominations cease." She plopped down into her seat with a whooshing thud and dropped her eyes to avoid making visual contact with the now-frowning president.

"I second the motion," Joy Henderson spoke up. The thought crossed Josie's mind that apparently Ms. Henderson is happy to vacate her post and is happy to help the pastor's wife succeed her. Then she did a double-take and jerked around to look at her grandmother. She raised her eyebrows when Eleanor turned to receive the silent inquiry. Josie was startled even more when Eleanor smiled slightly and ever so minutely nodded, then cleared her face again as her gaze returned to the front.

That was just enough time for Mrs. Glass to shake her head in disbelief and take a deep breath. She stiffly said, "The question has been called to accept the slate of officers, and as we all know, there is no voting on that question. So, we must proceed to the vote. Ballot takers, please distribute the ballots."

It didn't take long for the members to complete their ballots. Josie was wondering how explosive it would be if her grandmother actually beat out the incumbant. She didn't have to wait long as the ballot takers were swift about their counting.

Approaching the head table, the head ballot counter dropped a sheet of paper in front of the ladies' aid president, then slunk off to the back of the room. Then Mrs. Glass picked up the paper with furrowed brow and began to read the results.

"Your new officers are Gina Vizecky, Secretary; Cindy Van Meveren, Treasurer, and . . ." Mrs. Glass paused to catch her breath. Her face grew white and emotionless. "Eleanor Buchannon is your new presient. I will, of course, become your vice president, in accordance with the by-laws. In this position, I will make myself available to counsel the new president whenever she needs assistance." Not looking up, she added, "Let's sing the common table prayer before we eat lunch."

No one dared say a word, but launched into singing, "Be present at our table, Lord . . ."

Lunch flew by with many of the ladies' aid members stopping by the Buchannon ladies on their way out to congratulate Eleanor on her new position and wish her God speed. When the traffic slowed, Eleanor leaned toward Josie and said, "Let's go." They were nearly to the stairs when a gentle hand took Josie by the elbow. She turned to see that it was the choir director, Annie Citrowske.

"Please step into the choir room for just a second," Annie said. "I wish to ask you something."

"Go on ahead, Grams," Josie said, turning slightly back toward Eleanor. "I'll be right there." She then followed Annie into a nearby Sunday school classroom that doubled as the choir rehearsal room. "How can I help you?" she asked.

"I've noticed you've been attending church regularly; and now, you're here at ladies' aid," Annie said. She looked Josie in the eye and continued. "Your grandmother told me you sang soprano in high school, and I really could use another soprano in our church choir. Would you please consider joining?"

"I'm a little rusty," Josie said, wrinkling her nose. "I'm not certain you'd want me after you hear how I sing."

"Nonsense!" Annie exclaimed. "I sat in front of you in church last Sunday. Your voice is beautiful! Now, we rehearse Wednesday evenings at 7 p.m. right here in this room. Please come a few minutes early so that I can issue you a choir robe and your folder of music. There will be a slot for you to store your folder in that caddy near the door." She pointed in the direction from which they had come.

Before Josie could object, the voice of someone yelling came through the open window. Both women rushed to the window to better hear what the ruckus was about.

"I'm warning you, Eleanor, if you do anything to destroy the programs I've built up in ladies' aid, you'll be sorry!"

Josie took off like a rocket, taking the stairs two at a time to get to the parking lot before her grandmother and Mrs. Glass came to blows. Just as she reached the sidewalk, she saw the former ladies' aid president fling open the door of her Cadillac and jump inside. She ground the ignition and gunned the engine before spinning out of the parking lot so fast her tires spat gravel. Josie jumped in front of her grandmother to try to shield her from the flying rocks.

At that point, Annie joined the two women who were dusting each other off.

"Are you two alright?" she asked, making a fuss over them both. "Let me go report this to Reverend Van Meveren! That was uncalled for!"

Eleanor caught Annie by the forearm and stopped her. "Just let it go," she said. "Please? It must have been quite a shock to Mrs. Glass to have lost a position she has held for over ten years. And, one she has dearly loved and put a lot of time and effort into. Just let her cool off. It's the Christian thing to do—turn the other cheek, and all."

Annie heaved a heavy sigh and shook her head. "I don't know that I would be so understanding as you if I were in your shoes, but okay. If you say so."

"Thank you," Eleanor said, and gave Annie's arm an affectionate squeeze.

"Okay, then. Come on, Grams. I'll take you home," Josie said, taking Eleanor by the arm as the older woman let go of Annie. They paused breifly to say good night, and Annie went into the church as Josie helped her grandmother into the car and took her home. Enroute, Josie asked her grandmother, "What if Mrs. Glass doesn't chill out? What will you do if she really does try to get revenge?"

Chapter Four
Losing One's Head

Grams seemed hysterical when Josie took her call at work the next day.

"Slow down, Grams. I can't understand you," Josie said, swtiching the receiver to her right ear. "What happened?"

She heard her grandmother suck in a deep breath before going on. "There's been a tragic accident. Please come home immediately." Then she started sobbing.

"I'll be right there, Grams!" Josie hung up, grabbed her purse and briefcase and flew out of the office, barely leaving word with Vikki about going home due to an emergency. Josie hoped there weren't any cops on the road as she sped down Main Street to her exit. She was in luck, not seeing a Black and White Unit anywhere. Anywhere, that is, except the street in front of her house. There were three parked outside, along with one State Patrol SUV and what must have been an unmarked car as it had a portable flashing light on the roof.

Jose exited her ruby red Impala in record time and struggled through the crowd of news reporters and onlookers at the front door. Glancing into the living room where she saw nothing, she peered into the formal sitting room where she saw uniformed workers taking pictures of sheets of broken glass and what looked like a pool of blood on the floor in the sitting room. Josie didn't stop to question them, but urgently wanted to find her grandmother. However, she didn't have much choice. She couldn't spot her grandmother in crowded room. Josie started to plow through the cluster of people that was blocking her entry, but was cut short by a stocky uniformed police officer.

"What's your name, miss?" he asked brusquely. "Who are you, and where do you think you're going?"

Josie looked him up and down, and then stepped up to face him, nose-to-nose before answering. "My name is Josie Buchannon, and I live here. Where is my granndmother, and what is going on here?" She demanded. "And, by the way, who are you?"

"I am Officer Mitchell Bradley. See the name badge?" Officer Bradley was just a little crass for Josie's opinion. "May I see some I.D., please?"

"Actually, I was in such a rush responding to my grandmother's distress call that I forgot it in the car." Josie raised her eyebrows and added, "However, maybe that portrait over the mantel would serve the purpose."

When Officer Bradley turned to look at the portait of Josie, she quickly slid behind Bradley, cut through the sea of uniforms and found the center of attention. She nearly threw up. On the floor, lying in a pool of darkening blood, lay Gram's best friend, Virginia Fieney. Her shiny white hair was dulled brown by the brown liquid. Josie's fear nailed her feet to the floor. Her eyes were riveted to the lifeless body lying on the floor, about three feet from the severed head. Neck and head were still dripping blood. Josie felt woozy and collapsed into the arms of Office Bradley. She came to a moment later and asked what had happened, and, "Where's my grandmother?"

"Mrs. Buchannon is in the kitchen," Officer Bradley said and watched Josie fly in that direction. Fear pounded her heart against her chest as she ran down the hall. Her breath ran short. Finally, she burst into the kitchen where she found her grandmother seated at the table with a female police officer. Josie ran to her grandmother and threw her arms around her neck. Grams circled Josie's waist with her arms and squeezed tight.

After a few moments of silent consolation, Josie pulled back and searched Grams' eyes for answers. "What happened?"

Eleanor looked from Josie to the police officer seated across the table, whose name badge read Rodriguez. Her eyes implored the officer who nodded in acknowlegement. She cleared her throat and focused her attention on Josie. "Your grandmother has had a terrible scare today. As she and her friend, Viginia Fieney, were visiting, an unknown suspect threw a rock through the sitting room window. Normally this shatters the glass, but for some reason, maybe the angle, this time it just broke off a sheet of glass that acted like a guillotine as it fell inward at just the right angle as to slice through Mrs. Fieney's neck, effectively decapitating her." She glanced at Eleanor and added, "Mrs. Fieney died instantly without suffering any pain."

Just then a suited man entered the kitchen. He looked around and nodded at the police officer and extended his hand to Eleanor. Addressing the women, he said, "How do you do? I am Special Agent Freeman with the Federal Bureau of Investigation. We're taking over this case and will work closely with the local authorities to find the killer. I'm truly sorry for your loss. The crime cleanup crew will work all night to remove any stains and glass fragments from your living room. You will want to stay at a hotel or at a friend's or relative's place for the night. Just leave a phone number where you can be reached for questioning. You may come directly down to the police station for your statement tomorrow morning, if you don't mind."

The man took Josie's breath away with how fast he spoke and how straight forward he was, getting right to the nitty-gritty. Blinking she new there was something she wanted to ask him, but for the moment the question eluded her. Glancing at Eleanor, she noted that her gramdmother looked stunned. So, she turned back to the FBI agent, saying, "Yes, I'll make a few calls and get our overnight bags packed. How soon may we leave? I think I should get Grams out of here as soon as possible."

"Quite right!" the man in black agreed. "Well, then, if the local authorities have taken her statement and I can review it with her tomorrow, you may leave as soon as you're ready."

Ah! The question popped into Josie's mind and formed a clearer picture. She raised a hand and asked, "I recently worked with a couple of guys from your organization. Do you know Agent Malone and Andy Hoverstien?"

"Yes, I was told they had worked a case here a couple months back," Special Agent Freeman said, not blinking an eye. "They're currently reasaigned in different classified locations," he said without missing a beat.

"Yes, I'm sure," Josie said, understanding the necessity for secrecy in their line of work. She turned back toward the steps to go pack. She pulled her cellphone out of her slacks pocket and hit redial. P.J. had been the last one she had spoken to since Grams had called her work number earlier. It was listed first on the home phone's speed dial since Grams insisted on not calling Josie while she was driving, not being safe to drive and use the cellphone.

"Hi, Honey!" P.J. answered cheerfully. "Talk fast, I'm on my way to the men's room so I don't get busted for talking on the phone while at work."

"I understand, P.J., but there's been a fatal accident . . ."

"Oh, my God! Is your grandmother okay?"

"She extremely upset. Her friend, Virginia Fieney, died when a rock was thrown through our sitting room window. The window broke in half and sliced through her kneck. The crime scene cleanup crew is here and will be working all night. So, if it's alright, I'd like to come stay the night. I'll drop Grams off at another friend's place before I go back to work for a couple of hours, but I'll be at your place for supper."

"Of course! Then I get a home cooked meal, too! Please tell your grandmother that I'm very sorry to hear about her friend . . ."

"Thanks, P.J. Love you! Now, get back to work!"

"Love you, too, even though you're a slave driver!" They both chucked and hung up.

Josie called her grandmother's other best friend, the third in the Three Musketeers, as they called themselves. Alvina Fairchild answered, "Good morning! This is Alvina. How may I help you?" Ms. Fairchild had worked as a receptionist at the newspaper for over 40 years and still portrayed a professional appearance.

"Alvina, this is Josie Buchannon. I wish I could say it was a good morning," she said tentatively.

"Why, child? What seems to be the matter?"

Josie gulped and stammered, "I'm terribly sorry to break this to you, but Virginia died this morning, here at our house. And, Grams needs a place to stay tonight while the crime scene crew clean up our living room. Could she stay with you?"

"Why, certainly, dear. You may, too, if you like."

"I have a place. Thank you," Josie replied without elaborating. It may be a modern era they lived in, but in Lakewood, young couples don't openly live together. And, an elderly lady such as Alvina wouldn't appove of even one stolen night with a fiance, but Josie needed to be in P.J.'s arms tonight. Grams would be alright with Alvina because of how close the three-some had been. They may even want to reminisce about the past without an outsider tagging along.

With the logistics of tonight's lodgings settled, Josie went about packing Grams' and her own overnight bags. She took them and Grams' purse and rushed down the stairs with them. As she returned to the kitchen, Eleanor had just finished washing up her tea cup and was drying her hands on the towel that usually hung on the oven door handle. Josie set the bags down and enveloped her grandmother in another hug. Eleanor hugged her back, but pushed her away almost immediately. She seemed to have composed herself and was ready to leave.

Special Agent Freeman had disappeared, but Officer Rodriguez was still seated at the table. When she saw Josie in the doorway, she pulled a pocket-sized notebook from her jacket, along with a pen.

"Do you have those phone numbers for me, Miss Buchannon?" The officer was poised to write. Josie gave them to her; and, then handed Grams her purse. "Let's get going, Grams. I'll take the overnight bags." She picked up her keys, as well, and they headed out the back door and around the house to Josie's car.

Josie stowed the bags in the back seat and slid into the drivers seat while Eleanor struggled with the seatbelt on the passenger side. Josie reached over and snapped her grandmother's seatbelt into place for her; then, she took her grandmother's shaking hands into her own.

"Grams, I can only imagine how hard this is on you. Would you like me to stay with you at Alvina's? I can call P.J. and tell him you need me. He would understand."

Eleanor squeezed Josie's hands before she replied. "I'll be alright, dear. Alvina and I go way back. She has your cellphone number if things get really bad . . . as well as the hospital number . . ."

"Let's hope it doesn't come to that!" Josie said. She gently set her grandmother's hands down and took the steering wheel. As she drove the car down the street, Eleanor recited the Twenty-third Psalm, The Lord is My Shepherd. After that, they drove in silence.

Josie was able to deposit her grandmother at Ms. Fairchild's apartment without Eleanor breaking down. Josie thought about how strong her grandmother seemed to be. Then she remembered that Grams had had some practice in this sort of things when Josie's mom died. Josie's heart warmed at the thought that her grandmother was a Christian and that her faith comforted her. *I hope someday my faith will be that strong*, she thought.

Going back to work was a bust for Josie. Her thinking often strayed to the bloody stains on the carpet, which she realized would be gone by this time tomorrow. But, it was still a chilling thought. She did manage to reschedule her morning appointments for both today and tomorrow so she could take her grandmother down to the police station. And, she called their family doctor and asked if she could stop over to Ms. Fairchild's to give Eleanor a once-over, maybe prescribe a sedative for the coming night. The nurse who took the call assured Josie the doctor would be happy to stop by there on her way home from work. Josie heaved a sigh of relief. She was grateful they had such a caring physician in Dr. Debra Lindberg. This eased Josie's mind enough she actually was able to knock out a half dozen sketches for various advertising campaigns she had signed up the day before. By the time 5 o'clock rolled around, she was beginning to look forward to cooking supper for P.J., instead of picking up broasted chicken on the way over like she had originally envisioned. *I wonder if I packed anything sexy for tonight*, she wondered. It had been such a traumatic morning, she couldn't remember if she packed a toothbrush, let alone clean underwear for tomorrow.

Chapter Five
To Tell the Truth

Josie stopped at the local grocery store for a few things just in case P.J. didn't have everything she needed to make his favorite meal of pork chops, peas, mashed potatoes and white gravy, and chocolate cake with whipped topping. Not that that could happen, but you never know.

Before entering the store, Josie whipped open her overnight bag to be sure she had everything she needed in the line of toiletries and clothing. She noted that she had been very thorough in spite of the stress she had been under while packing. Perhaps all the practice she had had over the course of the past year, moving back and forth—to and from—New York City when she was working for Garvey, Sloan & Associates, LTD, and that one wonderful business trip she took to California with GS&A, had proven useful. She had been able to put the chore on autopilot earlier today. Nothing sexy, though. *Hmm. So like me to be practical, instead*, she thought, and went inside to shop for food. Picking out fresh ingredients for everything but the cake, she headed to the bakery. There would not be enough time to bake a cake tonight, especially if she wanted to spend most of the evening wrapped in P.J.'s arms.

Later, letting herself in with her key to P.J.'s apartment, she quickly unpacked all the groceries, started supper, and then went back to the car for her overnight bag. A dog howled in the distance making Josie shiver and hurry inside. *Keeping busy with the meal preparations and setting the tiny table would keep my mind off scary things*, she thought.

Soon, the lock on the door rattled with keys, and P.J. popped in the door. At the same time, Josie's cellphone rang. P.J. came over to give her a peck while she answered it. He cradled her from behind as she spoke into it, "Oh! Hi, Grams! Did Dr. Lindberg stop by? Um hm. Yes, I did call her. You had had quite a shock. You do exactly what she told you to do, whatever it was. Alvina has chamomile tea on hand? Good. I figured she would. I love you, too. Now, get some rest, okay, Grams? I'll pick you up at 9 a.m. tomorrow and take you down to the police station to finish up with the report, okay? Great. Bye."

Josie turned a 180 in P.J.'s embrace and wrapped her arms around his neck. He leaned down and kissed her soundly on the mouth.

"Mmmm," Josie said. "I can never get enough of that!" P.J. kissed her once more, rather quickly, and looked into her eyes.

"So, give me the details on what happened at your house this morning," he said. "How in the world did someone die because a rock was thrown through the window?"

Josie pulled away, went to the stove, and lifted the cover off the fry pan with the pork chops. The steam wafted upward and drifted toward P.J. Then, as she skewered the chops and transported them to a meat platter, she gave her fiance' all the information she had gleaned from the officials and from her grandmother.

"That's all I know," she said as she poured milk into two blue Tupperware tumblers. They sat down simultaneously, bowed their heads and recited the common table prayer. Looking up, P.J. caught Josie's eye and grinned his boyish grin. Her heart melted. She smiled back.

"I want to thank you for putting me up tonight. I would have felt like a fifth wheel at Alvina's. I know Grams probably could've used my shoulder, but—you know what?—she cried hard, but seemed to be taking it much better by the time we got to Alvina's."

"And, didn't I hear you say you called Dr. Lindberg to check on her?"

"Yes. That's the only thing that helped me keep it together at work this afternoon." Josie shook her head and watched P.J. dig into his pork chop. "So, what do you think?"

"I think some kid was out doing the Halloween pranks a little too early," P.J. said around his mouthful of food.

"That sounds plausible, but I was referring to your dinner!" Josie chuckled, P.J. snorted, then choked on a bite of food. He coughed and gulped down some milk. His eyes began to water; and his face turned red. But, he was grinning, so Josie knew he was going to be okay. She took a bite of her food while he settled down.

"There's cake for dessert. It has that whipped cream-like frosting . . ." Josie said. "I saw you have a carton of vanilla ice cream in the freezer, too. Would you like some with your cake?"

"Naw. The ice cream is old and almost gone. How about we take one piece of cake to the the couch and share it?"

"Alright. Just as long as you don't make me feed it to you!" Josie teased.

"How would you like to watch a movie?" P.J. asked. "I got this new one the other day. It's the latest in the Avengers series. Or, we could watch a rerun of Ugly Betty. I know you like that show. I don't know why, but if that's what you'd like to watch, I'll go along with that."

"The Avengers is fine!" Josie fake snapped. "I know you aren't a big fan of 'chick flicks'; so, we won't watch a rerun of one. And, for your information, I like Ugly Betty because it shows that plain girls with creativity can be just as successful as perfect models." Josie set the cake on the end table and pulled the afghan off the back of the couch. Sitting down near the end with the cake, she threw the shawl-like blanket over her legs. P.J. turned on the television, inserted the DVD into the player, and went to sit beside Josie.

"Are you going to want milk with this cake?" Josie asked. "You should have brought your glass over. And, you're not going to want popcorn, too, since we're watching a movie are you?" she asked. She loved to tease P.J. He was such a good-humored young man.

"Now wai—t just a minute!" He said. "Last time we watched a movie, it was you who insisted on having popcorn, with lots of butter, too, if I remember right!" He reached over and tickled her ribs. Josie had to put the cake back down for fear of spilling it. She shrieked with laughter at his administrations.

"Enough!" She managed, although it was getting hard to breath. P.J. stopped tickling her, per an agreement they had regarding tickling. Too much could make her hyperventilate. And, she had once read a magazine article about someone's baby dying because it was tickled to death. Literally suffocated having fun! Since then, she had made P.J. promise never to go beyond one, "Enough!"

After finishing the cake and the movie, P.J. put in another movie, one they had watched over and over because it was so romantic. They fell asleep in each other's arms before the movie was half over.

"Our God is an Awesome God" Josie's cellphone rang out. The sun was peeking in the apartment window, and it was time to get ready for another day.

"Oh, ow," she said, rubbing her neck and pushing P.J. off her.

"Huh?" P.J. grunted. "What's that? Is it Sunday and a church service is on?"

"No, but the TV is snowy because the movie finished. Please shut that off while I take care of my phone alarm."

"Okay," P.J. said and did so.

"You go ahead and shower first," Josie said. "I don't have to go into work until after I take Grams to the police station. I'll whip up some breakfast while I wait."

"Sounds good!" P.J. gave Josie a squeeze before trotting off down the hall. When he returned, dressed for work, Josie plated pancakes and sausages and took them to the table. "Let's eat!" she said, and sat down.

"Do you remember baking banana bread for me the first morning we met?" P.J. asked. He raised his eyebrow and took a swig of orange juice.

"Yes, I do. And, I remember you had to take it out of the oven because I was in the shower," Josie answered. "I also remember how handsome you looked lying on my couch. So innocent. I wonder what happened."

P.J. threatened to toss a pancake at her, and probably would have if it hadn't been doctored up with gobs of butter and a gallon of maple syrup. Instead, he just grinned and said, "What do you mean, 'What happened?' I haven't changed any . . ."

"No," Josie admitted. "If anything, you've gotten more handsome. Sexy, actually. What do you suppose caused that?" She wrinkled her forehead in mock thought.

"You know what caused that, if that actually happened." P.J. gave her a single upturned eyebrow. "Now, don't deny it."

"I won't, but you have to say it!"

"Alright, already! It's because I fell in love with the most wonderful girl in the world, and I can't wait to marry her!"

"So, what are you going to do about it?"

"Make her set a date!"

"Right now?"

"Yes, right now." P.J. took Josie's left hand in both of his. They both gazed fondly at the diamond ring he had placed there during a Reba McIntyre concert that summer. "I can't wait any longer, Josie! I need you to set a date now. Please? The guys at work are hounding me about when we're going to consummate our relationship!"

"Well, we can't have that, can we?" Josie thought briefly and said, "How about the first Saturday in April?"

"Next year?"

"Yes, this coming April. What did you think I meant? Five years from then?"

"No, but I was hoping maybe you'd give a date for this fall."

"First, it takes longer than that to plan a wedding. Second, I've always dreamed about an April wedding."

"Alright, then. April, it is."

"Just don't tell anyone until I tell Grams and you tell your parents, okay?"

"Okay. Now I have to get to work." Smack, he kissed her goodbye and left her to clean up the kitchen as well as herself.

Later, she collected her grandmother and her overnight bag and drove to the police station. On the way, Grams, being more clear-headed that the previous day, asked, "Did

I hear you right, Josie Girl, that you stayed at P.J.'s last night?"

Keeping her eyes on the road, Josie said, "That's right. We fell asleep on the couch watching TV."

"Well, if that's all you did, fine." Eleanor kept her eyes on the road, too. They had similar discussions in the past, and since Josie was an adult, Eleanor didn't want to pry, but she also knew that Josie knew where she stood on sex before marriage. It was taboo according to the church so it was taboo with Eleanor.

"On a happy note, Grams, P.J. and I set our wedding date! What do you think about the first Saturday in April?"

"That sounds like a beautiful date, dear!" We'll have to get busy booking locations and so forth, before that date is taken."

"Yes, Grams. I'm so excited!"

At the police station, Josie and Eleanor were escorted into the conference room where Special Agent Freeman and Officer Rachel Rodriguez joined them. They spent over an hour going over Eleanor's statement with a fine tooth comb.

"We apologize for the in-depth questioning, Mrs. Buchannon, but we wanted to make sure we got everything down, and if you had remembered anything since yesterday. We understand how upset you were. It would have been easy to have missed some detail that would be helpful in finding the perpetrator."

"Oh, I understand, too," Eleanor said. "I didn't want to relive it, but if it helps, I want to do it. I just can't think of anything else about the . . . uh, incident."

"How about prior to that day," Freeman asked. "Has anyone threatened you in any way?"

"Well, let me think . . ."

"Grams, what about the incident at the parking lot after the ladies' aid meeting?" Josie asked.

"Now, I told you to let that lie."

"What incident was that, Mrs. Buchannon?" The way Special Agent Freeman asked, it was more of a demand than a request. Eleanor didn't dare refuse to comply.

Sighing, she said, "I had just been elected ladies' aid president, and we were on our way out the door. Josie had been detained by the choir director and sent me on ahead. Outside, the outgoing president stopped me. She made a strong recommendation I don't mess up any of the programs she had put into place during her term. That's all."

"That's not all, Grams. Remember? She was yelling at you, and threatened you, saying you'd be sorry if you messed anything up. And, she actually squealed her tires as she left the parking lot.

"Plus, her husband, Mayor Ellis Glass, had been over a couple days prior to that," Josie continued, looking at the FBI agent. "He wanted to buy Grams' house, but she didn't want to sell. Whatever he said had Grams so shook up she called me at work."

"What was it the mayor said, Mrs. Buchannon?" Special Agent Freeman demanded.

Eleanor looked down at her folded hands. She seemed uncertain as to whether or not she wanted to share that information. Then she looked up and stated boldly, "That man got under my skin. You would think when someone says, 'No', she means it. He practically hounded me and said that he wouldn't give up trying to convince me to sell."

"You said the mayor and his wife both threatened you in one week?" Office Rodriguez asked. She furiously wrote notes.

Eleanor stared at the back wall, then said, "Yes, but I don't think either one of them would stoop so low as to throw a rock into my window."

"Not themselves, but a dirty official might hire some thug to scare you," Special Agent Freeman stated. That made Eleanor switch her focus to him. Her eyebrows hit her hairline in surprise. Josie's mouth dropped open as well.

Chapter Six

Investigations

"I'll get right on bringing those two in for questioning." Officer Rodriguez said. When Special Agent Freeman gave her a warning look, she said, "Don't worry. I'll be careful. I know we don't want to tip our hand."

After she left, Josie thought of something else. "I know they seem like the most likely suspects, Special Agent Freeman, but there were some shenanigans going on at Lakewood Technologies recently, too. Some creeps were pulling pranks at work, getting my finance' in trouble with his supervisor. That may not be anything, but he will soon be related to Grams. If someone is targeting the whole family, there might be a connection there."

"That certainly is another angle to consider," the FBI agent said. "We will investigate that angle as well. What's your fiancés name?" Josie told him, and they were dismissed.

In the car, Grams looked sidelong at Josie and asked, "I'm not certain that was the Christian thing to do, telling on the Glasses. I grew up with them, went to school with them, and even if the Mayor has become a bit greedy in his old age, I don't believe either of them is capable of pulling off such a stunt. Not even if he had it hired done."

Jose looked back at her grandmother with her eye brows lifted sky high, then put her eyes back on the road. She said steadily, "Grams, I've never known you to lie. And, concealing information is considered lying, even for the police, not just God."

Eleanor heaved a big sigh. "Josie, girl, when did you get so smart?" She reached over and stroked Josie's hair as if she was a little girl. And, just like when she was a little girl, Josie couldn't help but smile.

"Well, hopefully, the FBI agent now has enough information to at least get his investigation off to a good start." Josie said.

"Me, too, Pussycat," Eleanor said. "But, I don't know how much they will find out. Any little shyster could have thrown the rock. He—or she—wouldn't even need a reason to. Kids these days, as well as when I was a kid, didn't need a reason to get into mischief. Whomever did it, most likely never intended to hurt anyone, let alone . . ."

"Kill them. I agree," Josie said.

"*Our God is an Awesome God, He reigns . . .*" Josie flipped out her phone and answered. "This is Josie."

"What? Not again. Is it serious? Okay, we'll be right there. Huh?" Josie said. "Oh, I was just about to take Grams home from the police inquiry, but she'll come with. No problem." She hung up and looked at Eleanor and rolled her eyes. "P.J.'s in the emergency room again. Someone at work left a valve cover loose, and when he tried to tighten it, he got chemical burns all over his hands!"

Chapter Seven
More Trouble Brewing

"Should we call Special Agent Freeman with this information?" Eleanor asked as Josie turned the car at the next intersection to head toward Lakewood Memorial Hospital. "Unless someone gets stabbed or shot, the hospital won't do anything about it."

"Sure. Here, use my phone," Josie agreed. "I can't imagine what's going on at the Tech. It just doesn't seem right that so many mishaps are getting by the safety manager."

"Maybe he's involved," Eleanor said. "Hello? This is Eleanor Buchannon. I need to speak with Special Agent Freeman or Officer Rachel Rodriguez, in that order, please . . . Uh huh. I see. Yes, I'll hold." To Josie, she said, "Special Agent Freeman has left the office, but they're connecting me with Officer Rodriguez." Back to the phone, Eleanor said, "Hello, again, Officer Rodriguez. This is Eleanor Buchannon. I have another piece of information for you. P.J. Coleson just suffered another so-called accident at Lakewood Technologies . . . Yes, he's at the emergency room right now with chemical burns on his hands . . . No, I've never known him to be clumsy, just extremely conscientious and hard-working. Besides, I think he has more of an office job, not a manual one." There was another pause. "Thank you, officer. Yes, we'll call again if anything else comes up.

"Officer Rodriguez said she'd probably meet us at the hospital. She wants to interview P.J. about all these accidents, to see if they're related to our case." Eleanor still couldn't bring herself to say, "Virginia's death," or anything remotely related.

Josie pulled into a parking spot near the back of the hospital where there was a separate entrance for Emergency Room patients, caregivers and guests. Locking the car behind them, Josie went around to give her grandmother a hand up the steps and into the ER. Josie inquired at the reception desk as to which curtain she should go to to find her fiancé. Eleanor volunteered to stay in the tiny reception area and get a cup of coffee from the vending machine.

"Once we're done here, Grams, we'll all go to lunch," Josie said. "That is, if P.J.'s up to it." With that she left for the third curtain down on the left.

"Hi, Sweetie," she said, moving into the cubicle and giving P.J. a peck on the cheek. "So, what's the prognosis and what's the story here?"

P.J. kissed her back and held up his hands. There were blisters covering both of them, glistening with medicated ointment. "I had taken a report down to the floor manager and was heading back to my office when I saw something dripping from a valve in the corner. I ran over to see if I could tighten it, thinking it was water, or something just as harmless. I was calling for help as I twisted the valve to close it. Fortunately for me, the safety officer was right there with rubber gloves just as the liquid started to burn. Pushing me aside, he cranked it tight enough to stop the leak. By then, I was coughing and sneezing. My hands and nostrils were burning. That's when I figured out it was more than water."

"He was right there, with rubber gloves? That sounds too convenient if you ask me. Be sure to mention that to

Officer Rodriguez when she gets here. So, if it wasn't water, what was it?"

"Sulphuric acid."

Just then the nurse came in with gauze bandaging, a syringe, and a couple of prescriptions for P.J. She set them down and ran a plastic cup full of water at the nearby sink. Then she took out a pill and said, "Good, your nose has stopped bleeding. Wrapping your hands might hurt for a while, so I am going to give you a painkiller and a shot. The shot will work more quickly while the pill will catch up later. You'll want to take the rest of the week off of work like Dr. Wabasha said." P.J. was nodding throughout the entire lesson.

"I've already called my supervisor while you were out getting my prescription, so he knows not to expect me back until Monday," he said.

"Good. There! That does it." The nurse handed Josie P.J.'s prescription and his walking papers. She looked Josie in the eye and said, "You make sure this guy listens. We don't want to see him pop in here unexpectedly anymore. Oh! And, Mr. Coleson, no driving until after the doctor sees you for a follow-up next Wednesday. I've made an appointment for you at noon, so you can come on your lunch break. No showering until Monday, at least. If you can get assistance with a sponge bath or to sit in the tub and get help bathing without putting your hands in water, please do so. Otherwise, you'll just have to put up with yourself until you get back here."

"Yeah, I'm sure my co-workers will have something to say about it if I come to work smelling like I'm decaying." He looked helplessly at Josie and said, "Maybe my fiancée will help me out."

"I'm sure she will," the nurse said neutrally. As she left, Officer Rodriguez walked in.

"Hello, Ms. Buchannon, Mr. Coleson. Other than the obvious, how are you today?" Officer Rodriguez asked. "I see the doctor has had a chance to look at you and wrap up your wounds. Tell me what happened, and, start from the top." P.J. replayed his story for the officer. She let him talk uninterrupted, saving her questions for when he was through.

"Wasn't there a safety sign near the pipe indicating what was flowing through it?"

"The safety officer asked me the same thing; but, neither of us could find it. He said he would assign someone to make another one and put it up immediately."

"You let me know if you don't see one up when you get back to work. On the other hand, scratch that. I'll go check myself, then I can ask the rest of these questions of the safety officer directly. Thanks! Take care." The officer headed back out the door.

"Come on, P.J.," Josie said, "let's get you home. Grams and I can fix you lunch, and I'll feed you." She put the pills and the paper into her purse and reached for his elbow.

"Did I ever tell you how much I love you?" P.J. asked, pulling his arm away from her hand and putting it around her shoulders. She reciprocated by putting her arm around his waist.

"Only every time you see me, but I wouldn't have it any other way."

"Well, how is our guy?" Eleanor asked, rising from the bench as the two came meandering down the hall.

"I will be ju-u-ust fine," P.J. said, slurring his words a bit perhaps because the painkillers were kicking in. He nudged the exit door with his elbow and held it open for the women to leave the building.

"Grams, P.J. can't feed himself for a week. Is there any reason why he couldn't come home with us and stay in the guest room while his hands heal?" Josie asked.

"I don't see why not," Eleanor said. "I can keep an eye on him during the day while you're gone, and you don't have to pack up and move to P.J.'s and sleep on the couch."

"It's settled then," Josie said as she opened the car door and let P.J. ease himself in before she shut it. Eleanor took the front passenger seat.

Before putting her key in the ignition, Josie pulled out her cellphone and dialed.

"Who are you calling, dear?" Eleanor and P.J. asked simultaneously.

"I'm ordering take-out to pick up on our way home. You shouldn't have to cook all the time." She gave the man on the other end of the line her order and looked at Eleanor, who mouthed "The usual." She glanced at the rearview mirror and noted that P.J. had fallen asleep. She ordered him a cold submarine sandwich so she could refrigerate it until he woke up from his nap.

Once she got her fiancé, her grandmother and their lunch safely home and settled, Josie snatched one of the subs and headed for the door.

"I have a deadline at work, Grams! Please call me if you or P.J. need anything," she threw back over her shoulder. "But, I think he'll probably sleep all afternoon. Just leave him on the couch. I'll help him get upstairs later."

On her way back to the office, Josie dialed the church to tell the choir director she wouldn't be at practice tonight because of P.J.'s condition.

"I'm terribly sorry to hear about P.J.'s accident. I hope he heals quickly," Annie said. "And, it's unfortunate you can't be at choir tonight. But I suppose I can mention it to you over the phone. I'm planning a couple of solos for the holiday season, and I'd like you to try out for them."

"Are you sure you want to go there?" Josie asked, surprised. "I'm pretty rusty, and I'm still trying to fit in. What will your regular soloist say?" She really didn't want anyone hating her right off the bat because she was stepping on someone's toes. After all, look what happened when Grams was elected Ladies Aid President. Mrs. Glass really blew her stack and went so far as to threaten Grams. That was not a pleasant experience to watch let alone go through. Josie didn't have any more time to contemplate the situation as she had arrived at work. "Tell you what. You let me know when and where try-outs, and I'll try out. I can't say I'll be in it to win, but I will give it a whirl. If it works out, great! If not, just please don't ask me again, okay?"

"Fair enough," Annie said and made her goodbyes.

Josie's co-workers swarmed her office the minute she got seated. Everyone wanted to hear what had happened to P.J. Some reports indicated his hands were amputated. Others had him hospitalized, some even had him paralyzed from the waist down.

"Wouldn't that make for a horrible honeymoon," Jessica Springer said. Jes was planning her own honeymoon to take place immediately after she and her fiancé got married later this fall. "I just couldn't imagine going on my honeymoon if Joe were paralyzed from the waist down. What would the purpose of the honeymoon be if we couldn't consummate our marriage?"

"Yeah, Josie," Donna Schmidd weighed in. "I couldn't dream of even getting married until Snake was 'fully functional', if you know what I mean . . ."

"I do. And, I don't agree," Josie said. "If I love a man enough to marry him, you know there's a part in the vows that say, 'in sickness, and in health', right? That's how much

I love P.J. Fortunately, he's only burned his hands, and they will be healed by your honeymoon, Jes, long before ours." She gave them all the details she knew because, she knew if she didn't, she wouldn't get a lick of work out of them until they had badgered her into telling all, anyway. This was her family, her siblings, her co-workers. They shared everything. It got a little "Too Much Information" sometimes, like when one of the gals had marked her menstrual cycle on the bathroom calendar. No one really knew who it was, but rumors were flying until Josie finally sent a memo around asking the unnamed party to cease and desist airing her dirty laundry in the work rest room.

Jes flounced out of Josie's office in what looked like a tutu, always the fashionista. Donna slithered out wearing her black leather mini skirt again. Her punk-Goth personality had been unleashed after Josie took over, but she had more recently toned it down a bit. However, occasionally it still sneaked into her office attire. She hadn't been too happy when Josie had asked her to dress more professionally again. *Hmm, could she have been angry enough to throw a rock through our window?* Josie wondered. Josie really couldn't imagine it, but one never knew. She decided to keep an eye on Donna to see if her behavior changed at all. You never could tell about people. One day they're happy with you or your work, and the next, they're leaving bundles of magazines with your ad in on your doorstep or frozen gravy bags in your mail box. Go figure!

That reminds me, Josie thought. *I should call Officer Rodriguez and see if they ever found the pranksters who committed those practical jokes. That was kind of scary when that happened last month. Maybe they're related to the broken window.*

Chapter Eight
So Close and Yet So Far

Josie forced herself to focus on her work. It had been a distracting couple of weeks to say the least. It would be a relief when the authorities figured out who threw the rock into the sitting room window and accidently killed Virginia. Josie scratched her head with her sketching pencil, then shook her head to clear away unbidden thoughts. I can't make any money with empty sketch boards, Josie scolded herself. Then she applied the pencil to the blank page in front of her. She quickly outlined her next campaign for the new general store that was being constructed on the outskirts of town. The owner was capitalizing on the proximity to the freeway that came up from New York City. Peddler Jim's General Store promised downhome prices for some new and used-a-bit items that no home should be without. Jim Pepper brought in pictures of his inventory for Josie to use in the TV commercial he had asked her to create for him. He had a collapsible boat, cat ladders, antique horse tack and offbeat cookbooks. His line also included fishing tackle, nuts and bolts, tools and camping gear. Outside the shop, Peddler Jim said he would stock an antique pop machine that would offer 35-cent soda pop. Josie suggested he get an old-fashioned pickle barrel, too, to complete the picture.

"I'll go you one better," Jim had said good-naturedly. "I'll even bring in an antique pot-bellied stove to go with that pickle barrel!" This had given Josie the idea she was incorporating into the commercial. She sketched a picture of Peddler Jim rocking back on an old wooden folding chair, with his boots parked on the edge of the pot-bellied stove and a pickle in one hand, held like a cigar. She could just hear Jim's voice-over saying, "Come on in and set a spell. The fire's warm, the pickles are cold and the prices are ju—u—ust right!" Just a little shading with the colored pencils and the picture was done.

Josie sat up and held the board at arms' length, and was scrutinizing it when the intercom beeped.

"Josie, your grandmother is on the phone," Vikki piped in. "Line one."

"Thanks!" Josie said and picked up the receiver on her desk set and punched the lit up button. "Hey, Grams! Any changes in P.J.? What's wrong?"

"Nothing, dear. Just like you said, he's still sleeping soundly," Eleanor's calm voice eased Josie's worrying. "I just wanted to ask if you'd please bring home some ice cream or whipped topping when you get off work. I threw together an apple crisp and checked the freezer for topping, but there wasn't any. You choose whichever one you and/or P.J. prefer."

"No problem, Grams. Love to. Thanks for going to the trouble of baking. The apple crisp sounds wonderful! See you later!" Josie hung up with her grandmother, but remembered she was going to call the police station to see if they thought there may be a connection between their current case and the unsolved mystery of the strange presents.

When she got off the phone, she wasn't any closer to solving the mysteries than she was before. It seems the police had done very little with the pranks as they weren't able to lift any fingerprints off the packages. And, as long as the incidents were spread out and hadn't been repeated, the incidents were forgotten in light of more important cases. *Like Lew's death, and Virginia's,* Josie thought. She leaned back in her office chair and stared at the ceiling. The weird presents happened during the time Cassandra Coven was managing Sanderson & Sons. Josie tilted her head and screwed up her face in thought. *Those were just the type of things Cass would have done to try to scare me.* The thought jumped out at her. BUT, came the next thought. BUT Cass has been behind bars since then. She wouldn't have been able to throw the rock through the window. *Hmmm.* This will require more thought. Maybe Josie would run the idea past Grams and P.J. tonight over supper.

Supper! Goodness! It was past 5 o'clock and she still had to stop for whipped topping on the way home! Josie snatched up her purse and briefcase and flew out of the office and out to her car.

Josie walked into the house with the grocery bag dangling alongside her purse and briefcase. She couldn't wait to run her theory by her fiancé and her grandmother. Her two trusted confidantes would be able to tell her how crazy she was. A mouth-watering aroma distracted her from her thoughts long enough for her to peer into the living room and note that P.J. was no longer on the couch where she had left him. She rushed down the hall to the kitchen and threw the door open. There he was, seated at the kitchen table watching Eleanor dish up supper. She ran over to throw her arms around him and kiss him, but her packages got in the way. She tore off the bag, set it on the table, and dropped her purse and briefcase on the floor.

"Well, Josie, girl! Aren't you in a big rush!" Eleanor exclaimed. "Thank you for bringing home the topping."

"Mmm" Smooch. "Hi, Josie," P.J. said between kisses. "I'm fine! How was your day?"

Smooch. One more kiss before Josie let up. "Well, I managed to get down one good idea, anyway," she said. "And, came up with one doozy of a non-ad related idea that I want to run by you." She stripped off her suit jacket and hung it over the back of a kitchen chair. She went to the kitchen sink to wash up for supper, then sat down next to P.J. Normally, she would have set the table, but Grams had already done that. Josie flipped her hair back excitedly.

"So, let us in on it. What's with all the suspense?" P.J. yelped.

"Yes, dear. Out with it already," Eleanor added, bringing the casserole to the table. Josie could smell the garlic all the more, now that she was in the same room as the Italian dish she was about to devour. The tantalizing aroma compounded her excitement level. Her mouth watered in anticipation.

"Do you remember those weird deliveries made before Lew's death, the chicken gravy and the magazines?"

"Yes." Eleanor said. P.J. looked puzzled, so Josie brought him up to speed.

"When I first started working at the ad agency, someone left a stack of magazines on the front porch, near the door. It contained my first big-time ad. I thought it was an adoring fan trying to make sure I had enough copies to give one to each of my friends. The following month, a frozen packet of chicken gravy on the front porch, in the same place as the magazines had been."

"Whoever it was, never knocked," Eleanor interjected. "I would have been home that day."

"They had just left them there like some sort of psycho warning," Josie added. "Since we couldn't figure it out, at the time, we thought it was either a prank or a simple mistake. The fact that something like that happened twice, we figured we should call the police. When all these things started happening to P.J. I called them again. They said they had never solved the first ones. The perpetrators must've worn gloves, or something, so they never pursued them, chalking them up to childish pranks."

"Yes, I kind of figured that," her grandmother said.

"So, what made you think of it now?" P.J. asked.

"All the questions the FBI and the police have been asking about threatening messages from . . . whomever. Anyway, I was just reviewing my work this afternoon when it hit me. These unsolved weird pranks could've been done by Cass, who was, after all, trying to get rid of me not too long after that. So, what if she started doing these things before I became aware of them? Couldn't she have been the one behind the pranks?"

"Fascinating, Josie, girl," Eleanor said. "But, again, what does this have to do with our current, er, issue?"

"I haven't figure that one out, yet. But, there could be a connection . . . somehow."

"I know!" P.J. piped up. "I've seen a few detective movies where the suspect is behind bars, having an alibi for the time in question. Like Cass has an alibi for this most recent . . . incident. Anyway, in those movies, the suspect hires someone from the outside to do some dirty deed he or she is unable to take care of himself because he doesn't want to be involved. That's rich, hon! Cass committing a second murder from behind bars. You know, though; as bright as she was, I don't think mass murder was her style."

"Still, I wouldn't rule out anything too quickly," Eleanor said, the sound voice of reason. "Have you shared this theory with the authorities, Josie?"

"Not yet, Grams. I wanted to check with you first. If it's true, and Cass gets wind of my knowing, we could all be in danger."

The dinner conversation moved on to more pleasant topics once Josie promised to call Officer Rodriguez or Special Agent Freeman in the morning. They enjoyed Eleanor's apple crisp and the whipped topping Josie brought home, and P.J. and Josie settled down to watch a movie before going upstairs to bed. Eleanor left instructions for them to help themselves to more apple crisp, as a bedtime snack, and made her leave. Josie settled next to P.J. on the loveseat in the living room. The opening scenes of one of their favorite movies played on the television screen. P.J. lifted his arm to drape around her shoulders, and she was about to snuggle in for the night when he moaned.

"What's wrong, P.J.?" She pulled back and he dropped his arm like a lead weight.

"I think the pain reliever is wearing off. Hon, would you mind getting me another dose?"

"Of course not," she said and jumped up to get it and a glass of water. He took the pill and swallowed it with the water, grimacing. "E-ew! Those horse pills are bitter!"

"I'm really sorry, but I can't do anything about that! Well, except to get you some more dessert or to try to kiss it away!"

"I'll take the latter!" P.J. said as he wrapped his arms clumsily around her. He whined with the effort, but continued to hold her so she could administer her own kind of medicine. They nuzzled for a few minutes before P.J. pulled away and looked glassy-eyed at Josie. "I hate to break up the party, but I think those horse pills are stronger than they look. Or, is it, 'They're as strong as they taste'? Anyway, maybe we should get me up to bed before I fall asleep on the way up the stairs."

Josie agreed, and then helped him off the couch and up the stairs to the guest room. She pulled his work shirt off and drew his belt out of his pants before he slid back onto the bed. He was out before his head hit the pillow. Josie just shook her head, pulled off his shoes and covered him with the extra blanket from a nearby quilt rack. Leaning over him, she kissed his forehead and left the room.

Going to her own room, Josie stripped off her wrinkled blouse and tossed it into the clothes hamper along with her skirt and pantyhose. Unhooking her bra, she began to daydream about what it would feel like when P.J. would be the one to unhook her bra. Slipping into her pink satin pajamas, Josie was tempted to do without them for the night to see what it would be like to get into bed naked, something she may or may not like to do once she and P.J. were married. Too exhausted from the events of the day, she continued to pull on the nightwear and crawled into bed. She would have to imagine it in her dreams because tonight was not her wedding night. Thank God!

But the thought of P.J., injured, in the next room, kept her sleepless for a couple of hours. It gave her time to be creative about different scenarios for their wedding day and honeymoon. She thought she heard him moan once in his sleep, but he did not call out her name so she didn't get up. She turned her mind back to the question of the day: Could Cass have hired someone to throw that fatal rock, or had the Mayor done it as the authorities suggested?

Chapter Nine
Singing like a Bird

After helping P.J. with breakfast the next morning, Josie pulled on her gray trench coat over her red jacket dress and braved the October wind to get to work. Once she dropped her bags and hung up her coat behind her office door, Josie got on the phone to the police department. This time Officer Rodriguez was available to take her call. Josie outlined her theory and made the request to pull up the report she had made earlier that year regarding the mysterious deliveries. The officer agreed to check into it and get back to Josie if anything gelled.

The following seven days flowed pretty much the same as the previous day with one exception: Virginia Fieney's funeral. Because of P.J.'s injuries, Josie opted to come home from work early that day to stay with him so her grandmother could go to the funeral. He was still showing signs of sulfuric acid poisoning; and, his hands often hurt worse than the pain reliever was able to cover. Josie didn't want to leave him unattended for even an hour. Eleanor came home with a memorial bulletin in one hand and a soggy handkerchief in the other. Her eyes were red and swollen from crying. All Josie could think to do was to give her a hug.

"Please don't squeeze so hard, kitten," Eleanor pleaded. "You'll crack one of my ribs."

"Sorry, Grams. I just wanted to hug the pain out of you." She grimaced.

"I know, dear, but as you know, that won't do it. I appreciate the sentiment, though."

P.J. came over and gave Eleanor a quick, light embrace, keeping his hands extended as to not put pressure on them.

"Let's not cry anymore for Virginia," Eleanor said, shaking her head. "She's in heaven with the LORD and with her late husband. I'm sure she wouldn't want us to mourn her for long. Let's order in pizza and play some cards. Virginia really liked going to the senior center on Wednesdays to play Crazy 8. Let's have a game in her honor! Josie, you get the Dominoes, and I'll get the cards. P.J., find a chair you can slide into. I'll bring a soda with a straw in for you."

< * >

Josie hurried through her work every day for the rest of the week so she could get home and spoon-feed P.J. They would snuggle on the couch until he needed to take his pain reliever and crash into bed. Josie would be grateful when those bandages would come off; and, P.J. could resume showering. She didn't know how much longer she could stand P.J. without giving him a sponge bath, in spite of her grandmother's presence. It wasn't that she wasn't tempted, anyway. After all, she was human. She wanted to know every inch of her true love's body, in every way. But living under the same roof as her grandmother, a devout Christian, as well as her own Christian upbringing, Josie wasn't going to give in to her carnal desires, especially with P.J. being injured and under the influence of those pain killers that served as sleeping pills.

On Wednesday, P.J. was feeling better.

"Why don't you go to choir tonight," P.J. told Josie. "You've been a trooper helping me all week. You even stayed home from church Sunday to care for me. I love that, but it's time to get on with life!"

"Okay, okay!" Josie said, and teased him, "I get the picture! Now that you're better, you don't want me around anymore. Isn't that right? Hmmm?"

"You know that's not it! Come on, now. You don't need to miss anymore choir rehearsals or meetings, or church, or whatever, because of me. You cooked supper for me tonight, now let me do dishes and you get going. Or you'll be late!" He kissed her soundly, and then spun her toward the door. He smacked her behind and shooed her all the way through the door. She giggled like a toddler playing with a kitten, and then turned around for one last kiss at the door, before heading out.

That P.J.! she thought as she drove toward the church. *It's going to be so much fun actually living with him. Neither of us will have to get up and go home. We can just crawl into bed together! How sweet that will be.*

Inside the choir room, Josie drew her music folder from the slot and found her assigned seat. Annie and the other members had arrived earlier and were about to do warm-ups. The director tapped her music stand with her baton and said, "Your attention please. Last week I announced the try-outs for holiday solos. Those of you who indicated to me you would like to sing a solo will find selected pieces in your folders with notes attached. Next week we will start the try-outs. Please arrive a half an hour early, so we can do them before choir time. As that may not be quite enough time to complete the competition, the rest of you may come twenty minutes later than usual. We will continue rehearsal twenty minutes later than usual to make it up. Please pray for the contestants and that I may assign the appropriate solo for each winner. Thank you. Now, please open your warm-up books to page 83, and we will get started."

Josie thumbed through her music folder and pulled out the warm-up book as well as noting the folder contained four new numbers, not just one. There was one Thanksgiving, one Christmas Eve and two Christmas Day pieces. She would certainly be taking her folder home to look them over during the upcoming week. *Thank goodness Grams has a piano!*

After rehearsal, Annie caught Josie by the sleeve of her red suit jacket and pulled her aside.

"Wow! Red looks good on you!" she said.

"Thanks!" Josie replied. "What's up?"

"You may have noticed there are four solo numbers in your folder. I would like you to do all of them, but that would be unfair. You pick one that you really want, and it's yours. I still want you to audition for the others, too.

"Uh, uh!" Annie said and shook her head as Josie started to protest. "No 'buts'. I've been paying special attention to you these past couple of weeks. I know you say you're rusty, but you come through loud and clear. Well, clear, anyway. You have good pitch, clear tone and wonderful diction!" Annie took a breath and smiled. "I would consider it a privilege to work with you during the week if you think you need any help on any of the solos. Just call me, okay?"

Josie nodded, dumbfounded. Collecting her coat from the narthex, she went home with Annie's words of praise replaying in her mind. She was still floating on Cloud Nine when she drifted into the kitchen where Eleanor was making tea.

"Hi, Josie! You look lost in thought. How about some tea to get you ready for sleep, and you can tell me how choir went?" Eleanor asked.

"Sure, Grams. A good cup of tea to brood over is probably just the thing I need." She sat down and laid out the solo pieces Annie wanted her to consider.

"What do you have there, child? Special music?" Eleanor set a cup of tea in front of Josie, but off to the side to avoid the music. Then, she sat down with her own cup, next to Josie and pulled her bathrobe closer to her.

"These are solos Annie wants me to audition for. Well, for three of them anyway." Josie looked up at her grandmother and winced. "She told me to pick one I really like, and I didn't have to audition for that one, but that it was mine."

"Well, isn't that nice, dear? I always knew you could sing. I always thought you loved it, too. Why ever did you stop?"

"I went away to college, Grams!" Josie snorted, like her grandmother should have figured that out already.

"Yes, but didn't they have a college choir you could have sung with?"

"Yes, I think they did, but I was too wrapped up in getting my classes completed with high grades that I didn't feel I had the time to spend on something that wasn't related to my degree."

"Ah, yes. So, which songs do you have here? Are there any familiar ones? When is the audition?"

"The audition is next week. Let's see. The Thanksgiving number is just a soli—a small solo within a full choir piece." She handed it to her grandmother.

"'Come Ye Thankful People, Come', very traditional," Eleanor said.

"This Christmas Eve number is in Latin, Dona Nobis Pacem. It's not really up my alley to sing in a foreign language," Josie said, contemplating. "These other two look pretty promising, though." She handed one at a time to her grandmother.

"Yes. Let's go to the piano, now, and try out the melody," Eleanor suggested. Josie picked up the other music and the folder and followed her grandmother into the sitting room where the family Steinway was. Eleanor seated herself on the bench and Josie slid next to her. Eleanor used to accompany the choir herself, when she was much younger. She had no trouble picking out the melody on the first piece she set up on the music holder. Josie followed along and started singing, "The greatest gift of all, the gift of Jesus Christ."

"That sounds lovely, dear," Eleanor said as the last notes were fading away. "What do you think?"

"I think we have a winner. It's beautiful. I love the broken chord accompaniment, too. It sounds like snow falling in the mountains."

"Let's try the other one," Eleanor suggested. She plunged into a rousing rendition of Angels From the Realms of Glory, which led the two women to pull out other Christmas anthems and sing until they nearly lost their voices.

"Oh, my! It's nearly midnight!" Eleanor exclaimed.

"Ooh! And, I have to get up for work tomorrow!" Josie shouted. They both giggled, covering their mouths at the volume of it.

"Well, off to bed with both of us, then!" Eleanor said, shooing Josie away from the piano and up the stairs.

The ringing of the telephone awoke Jessica. Glancing at the clock, she was startled fully awake by the fact that she had overslept. It really wasn't surprising since she and her grandmother had been up so late singing choir numbers last night. But, who in the world would be calling at 8 a.m.?

No one at work would think to call her until she was a full half hour late. Josie threw back the covers and ran toward the stairs without putting on slippers or a bathrobe. Her lose fitting chenille nightgown fluttered in the breeze she created on her way down the steps.

"Hello!" she said, winded and relieved she had finally silenced the noisy communication device. *Why hadn't they called my cellphone number instead of the house phone?* She wondered.

"Good morning! Is this the Buchannan residence?" a somewhat familiar baritone asked.

"Yes, it is. This is Josie Buchannon. How may I help you?" By then, Eleanor and P.J. had already made their way downstairs and circled Josie with questioning expressions on their faces. Eleanor was fully dressed, but P.J. was still in the rumpled t-shirt and his boxers, having stayed over again. "Oh, hi, Special Agent Freeman. No, we haven't thought of anything more than what we had called Officer Rodriguez with the other day."

Raising her eyebrows and nodding her head, Eleanor stepped away to the refrigerator. She took out eggs and bacon and started to make breakfast, all the while seeming to keep an ear on the conversation. Every once in a while she would glance at Josie or tilt her head in that direction. She put on the kettle for tea and set the table. By the time she had turned the meat and taken the orange juice from the fridge, Josie had hung up the receiver and P.J. had wiggled a chair away from the table with his elbow and sat down.

"That was Special Agent Freeman," Josie said, rather unnecessarily. She sat next to P.J. while Eleanor reached for some glasses without taking her eyes off Josie. Josie continued, "As you may have heard, he just wanted to know if we had remembered anything new in the case. Of course, I let him know we hadn't remembered anything since my memory of Cass's behavior. He said the FBI had fully taken over the investigation from the local police. He said our idea was a good one and that he was sending someone out to the prison to question Cass." She paused, but when Eleanor and P.J. held out their hands for more information, she said, "That's it. They don't have anything new, either. After all, most of our neighbors work or were shopping or something when the accident happened. And, as you know, Lillie Butterfield next door sold her house to Mayor Glass a few weeks ago. She moved into a retirement home immediately after that. Her house has been vacant since then."

Eleanor put tea cups on the table and started cracking eggs. "I hate to say it," she said, "but, I'm afraid they won't catch the culprit. I hope and pray that person has a conscience and turns himself in."

"Me, too," P.J. said. He shook his head. "If I ever get my hands on that punk, he'll wish he had been the victim and not the perpetrator!"

"Easy, honey," Josie said, and rubbed her hand on P.J.'s shoulder. "Violence isn't the answer. A lot of kids throw rocks into windows to break them, not intending to kill anyone. Maybe that kid just wanted to scare Grams."

"I agree with Josie," Eleanor said. "It doesn't pay to hold grudges. The best outcome would be if this person would get the help he or she needs. Knowing Virginia as I did, she wouldn't want some young person to go to prison for the rest of their lives because of a horrible accident where a prank went bad."

Josie glanced up at the clock on the wall above the house phone. It read 8:20 a.m. She bounded from her chair and ran toward the stairs, yelling, "I'm late for work, Grams! Don't dish me up!"

That afternoon, Josie left work early again, this time to take P.J. to his follow-up doctor's appointment. The doctor removed P.J.'s bandages and gave him the go ahead to care for himself, and to go back to work. Once Josie took him home, again, P.J. happily sent her off to choir auditions so she wouldn't miss a beat.

Josie was shaking slightly as she entered the choir room. Annie was the only one there.

"Come in!" the choir director said. "Don't be shy. Let me just hang this sign on the door so that we won't be disturbed." Returning to the piano, she sat and looked at Josie expectantly. "So, which number did you choose to make your own? And, which others would you like to audition for?"

Pausing briefly to pull the pieces out of the folder, Josie said, "I would rather not sing Dona Nobis Pacem, but will do any number you tell me to. My favorite is The Gift of Jesus Christ, and I love the powerful melody of Angels From the Realms of Glory."

"Great! Let's hear you sing them both!" Annie said, and launched into the introduction of The Gift of Jesus Christ. Josie sang her heart out, and as the delicate melody wafted on air so did her spirit. It seemed to dance among the stars. She nearly felt snowflakes dapple her face as the piano keys tinkled the tune between verses.

"Awesome!" Annie cried, when the music ended. "You picked well. This song really suits you! And let's just give Dona Nobis Pacem a try. Please."

Josie twisted her mouth in contemplation. Finally, she said, "Okay." Grateful Grams had drilled her on all the pieces, she took a belly-deep breath and stretched her jaw while Annie started the Latin number. She had never studied foreign languages, and if she hadn't sung this in high school, she would have declined instantly. But, she handled the pronunciations fairly well and finished with the piano; so, she was thinking she hadn't totally shamed herself. When she looked up, Annie had tears in her eyes.

"Uh, I'm sorry if I blew it," Josie said tentatively, not knowing what to think about her director's reaction.

"Oh, no need to be sorry, dear," Annie said. "These are tears of joy. You can't imagine how long I've waited for a real singer to come along and take command of that piece. I thought I had heard you sing it at a high school concert a few years ago and was happy with it then. When you went away to college, I didn't have an opportunity to recruit you into the church choir. And, of course, when you did return to town, I had all but forgotten about it. Then you ran off to New York City and I couldn't talk to you then, either!" All this had come out in such a rush, Josie was stunned into silence. "When I saw you at the ladies aid meeting last month, it dawned on me, this was my chance!"

"What, exactly, are you saying?" Josie asked.

"I'm saying, Josie Buchannon, that you are a natural born singer, and that I hand-picked this song for you! Oh, I did think, if you were really shy, you'd have picked the soli in the Thanksgiving piece, but I was hoping you'd have a little more backbone than that and try something else. That would give me the edge I needed to have you do more than one!"

"What about Roberta Bates? Isn't she trying out, too? I'm sure there are more soloists, too, right? Shouldn't we each have one . . . a piece?"

Chapter Ten
Rubbing the Wrong Way

"Roberta sings passably well, but can be a bit stilted, overdone, and unfortunately, doesn't do foreign languages all that well. That's why I saved this piece for you. It's my favorite Christmas song, and it means a great deal to me if you would do this one as well as The Gift, and I want you to share the Angels song with Roberta, as a duet! And, she can have the soli in the Thanksgiving piece."

"And the other soloists?"

"There are no others who have signed up to audition," Annie said simply. "This is a small choir, as you have seen. It's all volunteer singers who blend well, but have no aspirations of grandeur. Well, except maybe Miss Bates." They both smiled at that. Josie felt her ears turn red and covered her face to hide it.

"So, will you do them—all three? Well, technically, two solos and a duet." Annie wanted to know. While Josie was turning it over in her mind, Annie added, "And, don't worry about Roberta. I'll take care of her. I'll make it sound like it was her idea, and I'll promise her more solos in the immediate future. In fact, I think she should do one on New Year's Eve and maybe another on New Year's Day . . ." Both women raised their eyebrows. *I wonder how many people actually come to church for those services*, Josie thought. *And, if Annie wants me that bad to go to all that trouble, I shouldn't let her down.*

"You sold me. I'll do it!"

"Thank you so much, Josie!" Annie came around from behind the piano to give Josie a hug.

"No. Thank you for having the confidence in me!" Josie accepted the hug with surprise.

"Okay. You have about ten minutes before choir starts. I'm sure Roberta is outside. I think I hear her warming up." Sure enough, a humming sound was coming through the door. So, Josie took her leave and went to the parking lot to call her grandmother on her cellphone to tell her the good news. She also called P.J. to tell him about the solos and to make sure he was getting along all right.

When she returned, she slid into her chair for rehearsal, hoping the rest of the chairs would fill up soon. She didn't want to be the only one in the room when Roberta came back from wherever she went to take her break. A few members had trickled in before Roberta came in and took a seat next to Josie, even though she normally sat two chairs away. As long as singers were seated in their voice section, Annie didn't care where they sat, so Josie didn't dare say anything about a seating chart.

"So, I hear we have to do a duet for Christmas," Roberta whispered to Josie. "We'll have to get together to practice . . . lot's. I'll be only too happy to give you some pointers."

"Thanks." Josie whispered back, not knowing what to make of it, but noting that Roberta already sounded a little stilted, perhaps insincere.

Roberta smoothed her pleated skirt and sat up straight for warm-ups. She kept her eyes glued on the director for the entire rehearsal while Josie had kept making side glances in her direction. Josie also noted that Roberta seemed to take great pains to sing every part louder than necessary, almost as if to drown out Josie's voice.

After rehearsal, Josie tried to leave without speaking to anyone. Out in the parking lot, though, Roberta caught up with her.

"Josie Buchannon! Are you trying to leave without setting up a practice time with me?" Roberta demanded.

"Uh. No. I just have to get back to my fiancé," Josie found an excuse. "He burned his hands at work last week, and this is his first evening alone without someone to help him . . . manage."

"So, you need to go home and help him unzip his pants so he can go to the bathroom?" Roberta said a little too loudly.

"Something like that," Josie whispered. "Please keep your voice down. It's been a long week, what with his accident and the investigation into the other one that killed poor Virginia Fieney."

"Yes. Poor Mrs. Fieney. She died in YOUR house. What a shame," Roberta said, practically cooing. "Be that as it may, we still need to set up a practice time. Let's meet at my place next Tuesday night. Bring your music and be prepared to work hard."

"Couldn't we meet here, at the church?" Josie asked, starting to feel a twinge of concern.

"What's the matter, Josie? Are you afraid to come to my home?"

"No, Roberta. Where do you live; and what time works best for you? I get off work at 5 o'clock most afternoons."

"No problem. We're in the phone book." With that, Roberta whipped around so fast her skirt twirled. She marched over to her own car and left, waiving and leering through the driver's side window.

Shaking her head, Josie moved to her own car and left for P.J.'s. She hadn't really been planning to actually go there, just to call and check on him before she went home. However, the fact that she had told Roberta she was going there made her duty bound to actually do it.

P.J. answered her knock on the door with a surprised but happy look on his face.

"You do care about me!" he said in a joking tone. "I thought you were just going to call me when you left church."

Josie gave him a peck on the cheek as she brushed past him on her way into the apartment. She dropped her purse on the end table by the couch and turned back toward him. P.J. had closed the door and followed her into the room so he took her in his arms as she turned and kissed her deeply. Josie's heart began to pound and her blood soared through her veins.

When they came up for air, she said, "I hope you never stop kissing me like that! I think that's just what I needed." P.J. kissed her again, this time his tongue pressed through her lips and danced with hers. She moaned. P.J. let up and looked her in the eyes.

"What? Was choir rehearsal really that bad? When you called me, you were ecstatic about getting those solos."

"I know, but the other soloist was pushy in rehearsal and almost attacked me in the parking lot. The division of solos wasn't my decision. Why was she so rude?"

"Josie, in a way it was your decision. You accepted the assignment when you were offered it," P.J. said as he took her by the hand and led her to the recliner. He sat down and pulled her into his lap. "So, maybe she's jealous."

"Maybe. Annie did say Roberta was about the only soloist the choir had. Maybe she is a little miffed."

"Ya think?" P.J. pulled her face to his for another kiss. His hands roamed her back, smoothing out the wrinkles in her navy blouse. She gave in to the pleasure of his administrations and quit talking about Roberta, choir rehearsal and music. She basked in the glow of their love as they pressed their bodies into each other. It wouldn't be long until every barrier could be stripped away and they could consummate the passion that was building within. She circled his neck with her arms and played with the curls on the back of his head while they necked.

All of a sudden, Josie yawned in the middle of a kiss.

"What's this?" P.J. asked. "Am I boring to you, now?"

"No. Oh, no, P.J.! It's just that it's been an exhausting week. Adding to it this dramatic evening at choir rehearsal and audition makes me one tired kitten." Josie borrowed one of her grandmother's nicknames for her.

"Then you had better head home before you fall asleep on me, or worse, yet, at the wheel." P.J. worked his way out of the recliner with Josie still in his arms. He carried her over to the door before setting her down on her feet. She reached for her purse and then back to kiss him good night. She sighed heavily and walked out the door without a word.

"Stay awake on the way home!" P.J. called after her, and then shut the door. He leaned back on the door and smiled. He was doing alright for himself in more ways than one.

Chapter Eleven

Brides and Bridesmaids

When Josie arrived at work the next morning, Vikki gave her a pouting face.

"That's some sour puss, there, Vikki! What's wrong?" Josie asked.

"We didn't get to do lunch last week and talk about your wedding. We need to reschedule."

"You're right. How about today?"

"Great! Let's go to Deer Valley to that great little café! They're serving my favorite dessert!"

"You're on! Now, how about my messages?" Josie collected just two as she walked by Vikki's desk. They shared a wink, and Josie kept walking. She greeted the office staff individually as she did every day. Jessica Springer stopped her as she came parallel to her desk.

"So, Josie, are you and P.J. coming to my wedding next Saturday? Jimmy and I haven't gotten your RSVP yet. I know you've been busy lately, but I do need a head count by Monday."

"Ah, yes! I'm so sorry Jes! So many things have happened lately! But, of course, we'll be there! We wouldn't dream of missing it! Who's playing for your wedding dance? If they're any good, maybe they'll play for ours."

"Great! And, The Happy Wanderers will be playing. They play Country Music and some cross over stuff. I'm pretty sure you'll love them."

"Super. I'll be looking forward to hearing them." Josie nodded; and, smiling, she went on to her office in the back. Booting up her computer, she checked her email and her daily schedule. Right there in black and white was a calendar reminder to ask the staff to participate in the wedding. There weren't any details since she had posted the reminder two months earlier; and, she wasn't entirely certain how many of them would still be around after Cass was gone and college resumed for the fall. But, everyone stayed, so it was time to make some decisions.

Josie took a stenographer's notebook out of a desk drawer and picked up a pen. She tilted her office chair back and tapped the pen on her mouth. After a moment's thought, she made her list:

> Vikki Dale—Maid of Honor
> Jessica Springer—Bridesmaid
> Donna Schmidt—Bridesmaid
> Hildy Shoemaker—Bridesmaid
> Patty Coleson—Bridesmaid
> Pauline Coleson—Bridesmaid
> Nathan Danielson—Usher

Josie got on the office telephone and called Jessica into her office.

"What's up, boss?" Jess said, flouncing onto the couch under the window. "Did I do something wrong? Or, do you have a modeling job for me?"

"No, nothing of the sort," Josie said and smiled. "I had an interesting reminder on my schedule for today. It is my happy pleasure to ask you to be a bridesmaid in my wedding. What do you say? Will you stand with me on my wedding day?"

Josie saw Jessica's eyes light up. She leaped off the couch and hooted. "You bet! Woo hoo!"

"Please, keep this under your hat until I've had a chance to ask everyone else, too, okay?"

"Okay, okay! But you'd better do it fast! I'm not good about keeping secrets. And, Josie, you know if I didn't have six sisters, I would have asked you to be in my wedding, too."

Josie smiled and waved Jessica off. "Don't worry about it Jes. I didn't expect to be asked since we haven't known each other for more than, what, almost a year? Even so, you're like a sister to me, since I don't have any. Thank you for saying 'yes'. Now, go back to work!"

"Yes, Ma'am!"

Next on the list was Donna Schmidt. Josie keyed in her desk number and invited her into the office.

"Hey, Josie! What's Jessica all smiley about?" Donna asked as she chose to lounge in the canvas chair in the corner.

"Because she said 'yes' to the same question I'm going to ask you."

"Oh, yeah? What?"

"Will you be my bridesmaid?"

"Sure, why not? Just don't get too much of a frou-frou dress, okay? Nothing hot pink, see. Red is more my color."

"Ooh, aren't we picky?" Josie teased. "Actually, April's shade of pink would probably be more icy, but we'll see what's available. Oh, and mum's the word until I ask Hildy, okay?"

"If you say so."

"Thanks for saying 'yes'!"

"Hey, no problem. Catcha later."

Josie went back to her phone for another call, but it rang before she could dial Hildy's number.

"This is Josie. How may I help you?"

"Hey, it's me, P.J." He was calling in on her private line.

"Hi, honey. What's up? You didn't get hurt again, did you? Do I need to pick you up at the emergency room?" The hair on the back of her neck stood straight. Red flags were going off in her head.

"No, I'm fine," he said, chuckling. "I was just thinking about my family and friends, and noticed I'm a little short on male members to fill our wedding slots. Do you know anyone we can ask to be an usher with one of my college friends?"

"What a coincidence! I was just asking the females on my staff to be bridesmaids! That actually leaves one male member of the staff without a job. Let me ask Nathan if he would do us the honor of being an usher."

"Sounds good, sweetie," P.J. said, and they bid each other good day.

Josie had to look up Nathan's extension number as she seldom called him. He usually just caught her in the hall or at a meeting. She wrote his number down and went back to calling Hildy first.

Hildy walked into the office with a scowl on her face. She stood in front of Josie's desk until Josie ordered her to sit down. Sliding the hardwood-folding chair to front and center of Josie's desk, Hildy sat stiffly. She crossed her sweatered arms and her corduroy legs and glared at Josie.

"This better be important," she said. "You know I hate to be interrupted when I'm in the middle of a project."

"Yes, like the time you put together a whole TV commercial when all I asked you to do is if you could turn a character inside out!" Josie giggled. "Remember how Cass went ballistic?"

Hildy couldn't help herself. She snickered, too.

"I can't believe she didn't blow a gasket, right then and there," Hildy said, rolling her eyes and unfolding her body. She leaned forward, her hands on her knees. Peering sideways at Josie, she said, "How can I help you?"

"I would very much like to have you in my wedding. Hildy, will you be one of my bridesmaids?"

"Na, hunh uh. No way am I climbing into a dress and parading down the aisle with flowers in my hair."

"I promise not to get dresses that are too 'frou-frou' and you don't have to wear flowers in your hair," Josie begged.

"I look like a cow in a dress. Never, no way will I wear a dress! Isn't there something else I can help with that doesn't require wearing a dress? I'd love to be in your wedding, but how about something like personal attendant? They aren't expected to wear a dress, are they?"

"Not really, I guess. I've seen some wear dressy pantsuits or split skirts or the like. You know, I hadn't thought about a personal attendant. If I get a fancy, puffy long dress, I will need someone to help me go to the bathroom. Are you okay with that?"

"Yeah, I guess so."

"Personal attendants also help with hair and makeup and dressing the bride. How about those duties?"

"I might not manage a curling iron very well, but the rest of that I'm okay with."

"Then, I suppose I can get a hair appointment the morning of the wedding, so you won't have to worry about the curling iron bit."

"Well, then, you have a deal. I will be your personal attendant." With that, Hildy got up and went back to work. Josie took a minute to collect her wits about her.

She had never ever heard of anyone ever turning down an opportunity to be a bridesmaid just because they didn't want to wear a dress.

"Huh!" She snorted. "Go figure!" Then she pulled over the paper on which she had jotted Nathan's extension and dialed it. Nathan seemed to arrive in her office before she had replaced the receiver.

"Yeah, boss? What can I do for you? Just name it." Everyone called her "boss" after Cass had been arrested. It was like an in-house joke because Josie used to call Cass that, and Cass just ate it up, actually preening when she heard it. It was like lifeblood to Cass to be the one in power. And, while Josie could be decisive and was a good business manager, she was nothing like Cass. Josie did not wield an iron fist. She showed genuine concern for her employees and treated them all fairly. It took Josie all this time, since Cass had been arrested, to hear the term without wincing.

"Hey, Nathan. How are you today?" Josie asked, even though she had just asked him that twenty minutes before when she first arrived. Nathan didn't seem to notice. He just smiled and said, "Fine, thank you."

"Nathan, P.J. just called and said we need another usher for our wedding party. We would love it if you would be one of our ushers. Would you, please?"

"Have you set the date, yet?" Ever the number cruncher, Nathan asked the one question the ladies had neglected in their haste to accept. Josie told him, and he said, "Yes, I believe I'm available that day."

"Of course, we would love to have your wife and children as guests, as well," Josie was quick to add. "I'm sure they'd love to dance with you all dressed up in a tux."

"Thank you! Yes, they probably would. Just let me know when and where to get fitted for the tux. I'll be there."

"Yes, we'll keep you posted. Thank you!"

"If there's nothing else, may I be excused to get back to work?"

Josie smiled and nodded. And, just as quickly as he arrived, Nathan disappeared. Josie blinked her eyes and grumbled something about Superman before calling P.J. with the results of her requests. Then she went to work herself knocking out a half dozen campaigns by noon when Vikki paged her.

"Are you ready for lunch?" the perky receptionist asked.

"More than ready. I'm famished!" Josie answered. She picked up her purse and grabbed her sweater. On the way through the work room, Jes stopped her again, handing her a canvas tote with what looked like magazines inside.

"Vikki mentioned you two were going to talk about the bridesmaid dresses over lunch today," Jes said. "Here are some *Brides Magazines* and catalogs for you two to look at. I even marked some I liked for my own wedding. Stay away from the one I have a heart around, though. My girls are wearing them next week!"

"Thanks!" Josie said and accepted the offering. Then she and Vikki ran out to Josie's car and headed up the road to an hour of fun, food, and friendship.

They decided Jes had great taste and selected two for the girls to look at when they got back to the office. By then, their food had come and they settled in for a little harmless gossip while they ate.

< * >

After a week without Jessica at the office, the staff was starting to show some frazzle. By Friday, they were all pulling their hair out and getting short-tempered. Josie had never realized how much they all depended on the ebony goddess to keep their spirits up as well as do their research and modeling for advertisements. By noon she had had enough of the petty complaints and unnecessary disruptions. She got on the intercom and called a staff meeting. Once everyone was seated in her office, she laid out an ultimatum.

"This is the deal, I will order in pizza, IF we can all get along for two more hours without killing each other. After two hours of solid work, we'll meet in the conference room for reports. IF we have accomplished enough work for the day, anyone who wants to take a couple of hours vacation pay, or go home without two hours of pay, may do so. This is an exceptional occasion. I would think hard before answering. This opportunity may never come again.

"While you consider my proposal, I have to admit, I haven't had time to go shopping for Jes and Jimmy's wedding tomorrow. I will be leaving at 2 p.m. to do so. So, I will not be here to monitor your fighting after that time. Now, anyone else willing to admit they haven't as yet gotten the bridal couple a gift is welcome to go in on mine. Does anyone have any suggestions as to what to get, or should I just go to Shopko, where they are registered, and get something off the list?"

No one spoke up; so, Josie sighed and said, "Shopko, it is. Now, who's on board with my original proposal to work hard for two hours and go home?" All hands went up. Decision made.

Thirty hours later, Josie and P.J. were wearing their navy Sunday suits and heading to The Church of the Holy Name in Deer Valley. Josie had been able to find one item left on the Shoko list, but had trouble wrapping it. The white satin duvet wouldn't fit in the largest gift bag she bought. She had had to run up to the local general store to find a box big enough and gift wrap in a quantity that would fit the box, then cram the duvet into the box before wrapping it. Now, it took up most of the back seat of P.J.'s Cougar.

They decided to leave it in the car until they arrived at the reception at the Deer Valley Community Center.

At the church, Josie and P.J. were ushered to the bride's side. The pews were decorated with pumpkin colored rosettes. Soft organ music played in the background. Then a violin joined in. Soon, the marriage ceremony started. The priest came in and invited the congregation to rise. Josie looked around and admired the bridesmaids' dresses as they came up the aisle. They were the same rust colored ones with the heart drawn around it in the catalog Jes had lent to Josie. They had empire waists, ruffled chiffon sleeves and a scoop neck. The skirts were long and straight. Each bridesmaid wore orange sequined flip-flops instead of the traditional dyed-to-match pumps. *Jes always was a fashionista!* Josie thought. Not to mention flip-flops would be easier to dance in later. Josie noticed something else about what the bridesmaids were wearing: Each girl had on a matching pearl necklace with an amber bejeweled slide and coordinating pearl earrings. Josie remembered Jes had mentioned buying them each a set as a bridal gift.

Suddenly, organ music changed pitch and volume with a fanfare that drew everyone's attention. Then the organist launched into the traditional Bridal March. Cameras flashed as guests took pictures of the bride in the doorway with her father. Josie sighed. *I hope I look that beautiful on my wedding day!*

Josie's eyes followed Jessica up the aisle and into the arms of her groom. Jimmy was resplendent in a chocolate malt colored tuxedo with dark chocolate satin trim. His cream-colored ruffled shirt was tipped in dark chocolate; and, his shoes were patent leather, also in dark chocolate. The color combination made his skin gleam like cinnamon. His groomsmen were dressed in the same tux; but, were missing the cummerbund that Jessica must have insisted Jimmy wear.

"Can you picture us up there?" P.J. whispered in Josie's ear as they sat.

"Yes, but in sky blue!" Josie answered, also in a whisper. P.J. raised his eyebrows and smiled. He squeezed her hand and returned his gaze to the bridal party. Josie couldn't wait until the dance. She was certain she would be floating a foot above the ground with P.J.'s arms around her.

Chapter Twelve

No News is Good News

Jes and Jimmy's vows went smoothly, as did the simple, but filling reception meal and the swinging dance. Josie and P.J. agreed that the Happy Wanderers were awesome and went up during a break to speak to them about playing for their own wedding dance in April. Luckily, the ensemble was still available. Throughout the evening, Josie was glad she opted for a simple, street-length sheath and matching flats to wear to this wedding and dance. As much as she and P.J. were out on the dance floor, any longer of a skirt, or higher a heel, she would not have been able to last the night. As it was, the navy jacket dress came in handy.

Sunday morning dawned too early for Josie. She and P.J. had helped close down the dance, coming in after 1 a.m. that morning. She had left a note for Grams not to wake her for 8:30 a.m. church service, which they were accustomed to attending. Instead, she would take in the 11 o'clock service after Bile Class. By the time she returned home, Eleanor would have lunch on the table. *I'm so glad Grams is so understanding and supportive* Josie thought as she showered for church. She let the hot water pelt her back and neck a little longer than she had anticipated and ended up having to rush through the rest of her preparations. In a hurry to get out the door, she had forgotten to pick up an offering envelope from the hall desk. *Oh, well. God knows what I give, even if it's just cash in the offering plate.*

After church, Josie stopped by the convenience store to pick up a Sunday paper. The New York Times had a banner worth stopping for; and, she nearly tripped on her way to the checkout because her eyes were glued to the paper. It read:

> Coven court date set,
> *Prosecutor claims tight case*

Jose couldn't wait to get home to read it; so, she sat in her car, which was parked at the side of the convenience store, and read it. The article stated Cass's court date was in about two weeks at the county seat. It was scheduled to begin at 10 a.m. Josie began to anticipate a call from the District Attorney's office in regards to testifying for them. She jotted the date, time and location into her datebook. She wasn't going to miss this. *P.J. has to hear about this!* She pulled out her cellphone and dialed his number.

"Morning," came through the receiver, somewhat muffled.

"P.J. Coleson, you get your lazy butt out of bed. What would your parents say about you missing church this morning?" Josie wasn't about to let him get soft on her. And, he'd better not miss any choir performances, either, or she would give him what—for!

"Sorry, Josie," P.J. sounded clearer now. "I woke up with a sinus headache, took two sinus pills and went back to bed. I'm awake now, thank you. What's up?"

"I'm sorry, P.J. I shouldn't have yelled at you," Josie apologized. "It's just that the Sunday paper has listed Cass's court date as next Tuesday. And, I should be getting a call from the D.A.'s office any day now to let me know when I have to testify."

"The time has finally come, huh? What's the date?"

"October 31. P.J., please come over for lunch. I need you to hold me. Plus, we can put some more touches on our wedding plans."

"Okay. Give me a few minutes to shower quick, and I'll be over."

P.J. must have flown through the shower like it was a supersonic space-age one aboard a starship because he was there in what seemed like 15 minutes. Josie hadn't yet had time to boil water for tea. She figured a little chamomile tea to calm her nerves would be just what she needed after reading the article on Cass's court date. P.J. sat down at the table, running his hands through his still-wet hair. Wet or dry, Josie loved looking at his hair, his crystal blue eyes and his ready smile. She couldn't wait to marry this man because she wanted to be around him 24/7, 365. She bent over and kissed his forehead. P.J. grabbed her around the waist and pulled her to him.

"You're not getting off that easy!" He told her, and wrapped his arms tightly around her and planted his lips on hers. His mouth felt searching. Her lips met his with the answer: Yes, she needed him. She needed his strength, his presence, and all the love he could give. She didn't want to face her former adversary alone, and she wouldn't have to. As an eyewitness to the event that Cass tried to shoot Josie, P.J. would also be testifying. Josie relaxed in his arms as much as possible in the somewhat awkward position of practically lying on her back in his lap. Her arms slid up P.J.'s shoulders and linked behind his head while the rest of her melted into his chest. Her pulse sped up and her ears flushed.

Suddenly, she was brought back to reality with the whistle of the teapot. They broke the kiss with a smack of suction releasing. Josie opened her eyes and slowly righted herself and got off P.J.'s lap. She straightened her navy turtleneck as she rounded the kitchen table and reached for the teapot. Shutting off the stove first, she proceeded to pour two cups of hot water and replaced the pot on the stove. She pushed the tea caddy toward P.J. with one hand while pulling out a chamomile with the other. She tore open the packet and dropped the inner gauzy bundle into her cup. She wouldn't blame P.J. if he also chose chamomile tea, however he was already tearing into a spiced chai.

"So, where's that newspaper article that has you all frazzled?" he asked, pouring milk and sugar into his tea. "Was there anything about us testifying?"

Josie snatched up the paper from the counter near the sink and dropped it on the table in front of him. P.J. read the article out loud, determining that no names were given, just that the district attorney had eyewitnesses that would testify against Coven in the attempted murder of Josephine Buchannon, as Cass would be tried for both cases, one murder and one attempted murder, at the same time.

"Nothing to fear, my dear," Eleanor said, entering the room. She looked in the peak of health in a rose pink slack outfit and matching suede loafers. She went to the stove and got her own cup of hot water.

"Grams, I could have done that," Josie complained.

"You sit, dear. I'm sure you have enough on your mind, having to give your statement in court this week," Eleanor answered. "Just remember, there were plenty of witnesses and her attempt on your life was also recorded. It's an open and shut case."

"All they need to do is find that Viagra bottle with Cass's fingerprints," P.J. said, "and she's toast! Speaking of toast,

I don't suppose you have some bread and peanut butter I could toast for a quick bite to eat?"

Josie got up faster than Eleanor who had sat down during the conversation and started to enjoy her tea. Josie even popped the bread into the toaster for P.J. While they continued talking about the case, the telephone rang. Already up, Josie answered it. Her eyebrows flew upward as she listened to the voice on the other end.

"What did you say?" she asked several times. "He's right here. Would you like to speak to him?" (pause) Apparently the caller wanted to speak with P.J. "P.J. it's for you. It's the D.A.'s office." P.J. stood and took the two steps it takes for him to cross that small kitchen. He relieved Josie of the telephone transceiver and took over the conversation with the person on the other end of the line.

"They were able to bump up the time of the court case from 2:45 p.m. to 10 a.m.," Josie said softly to Eleanor. "They want us to start taking the time off work and working with our attorneys to review our testimonies." Eleanor just nodded, keeping quiet so P.J. could hear the person on the other end. The women quietly sipped their tea until P.J. finished his conversation. When he finished, he returned to the table.

"We're setting a meeting time for Thursday at 5 p.m.," P.J. said, looking at Josie. "You can get off work 15 minutes early, right?" Josie nodded, juggling her schedule in her head.

"That should work," she said, then looked at Eleanor.

"Don't worry, dear," Eleanor said before Josie could ask. "I'll throw a casserole in a little later than usual. It'll keep until you two can get away for supper. Just come here when you're done with the D.A. I'll wait for you."

"Thanks, Grams!" Josie said, and gave her grandmother a sideways hug.

"No problem, dear. And, speaking of food, let's get something going now!"

< * >

On Thursday, Josie picked up P.J. at work since she was able to get off work at 4:30 p.m. *It never ceases to amaze me that, being my own boss, I can set my own scheduled,* Josie thought as she pulled into the parking lot at Lakewood Technologies. She found an open spot two spaces down from P.J.'s electric blue Chevy Cruise. She had brought along a professional magazine to browse through while she waited for her fiancé to come out of the building. She had just perused the index and thumbed to the one article she wanted to read in the whole magazine when the passenger door of her car opened. She threw the magazine into the backseat as P.J. slid into the seat beside her. They greeted each other with a quick peck on the mouth.

"How was your day, honey?" Josie asked P.J. as she started the car.

"It was great up until 4:30 p.m.," P.J. answered as he buckled his seatbelt.

"What happened then," Josie asked, taking a quick glance at P.J.

"Mr. Williams called me into his office to give me a verbal warning. He said he realized the accidents I've been having weren't my fault. At best, they were just that, accidents. However, he told me to use the inter office messaging service from now on. If he caught me in the plant part of the building again, he would write me up! Imagine that! I've done nothing wrong except to be in the wrong place at the wrong time—becoming a victim, no less—and, I'm the one in trouble!"

Chapter Thirteen
Counselors and Counseling

"Your boss must have given you that warning for your own good, P.J. He doesn't want you to get hurt anymore."

"I suppose. Maybe the company can't afford anymore E.R. charges, either."

"Plus, if you're not in the plant, those hooligans can't pin any more accidents on you," Josie said as she pulled into the parking lot of the restaurant at which the D.A. asked them to meet him. The couple got out of the car and entered the restaurant. They found the maître de who knew exactly where to seat them, in a secluded corner of the back room where there were no other customers eating. They ordered water with lemon slices and looked over the menu for something to do while they waited.

Presently, a navy-suited man with ink black hair and a leather briefcase approached their table.

"Hi, are you Josie Buchannon and P.J. Coleson?" The couple nodded. "Great! I'm Derrick Baldacci from the District Attorney's office." They shook hands; and, he sat down. Mr. Baldacci pulled a file and a legal pad from his briefcase and a pen from the inside pocket of his suit coat.

Just then, the waitress came back with Josie's and P.J.'s water. She asked what Mr. Baldacci was having. He ordered black coffee; and, she went away to get it.

"According to your statement, Mr. Coleson, when you entered Miss Buchannon's office, Ms. Cassandra Coven was pointing a gun at Miss Buchannon. Do you know what kind of gun it was?"

"A hand gun, is all I know. I don't know much about guns." P.J. answered.

"Can you describe it?"

"It looked like guns I've seen in Western movies, the kind cowboys shoot. Does that help?"

"Yes, that is fine," Mr. Baldacci said. Then he looked at Josie.

"Did you know Ms. Coven was going to be in the building that night?"

"No, not for certain. I had been working with the FBI on setting her up to show her hand. I—I—I was bait." Josie finished softly. She didn't want to think about it. After it was over, everyone said she had been brave, courageous, a real hero. She hadn't felt like a hero. She felt lucky to be alive. She hadn't really wanted to be put in harm's way, but she didn't want Cass to get away with murdering their boss, either. Plus, there was some small part of her that wanted revenge for all the deceitful things Cass had pulled as the manager of Sanderson and Sons. *That red-headed witch is going to get her come-upings,* Josie thought. Then another thought struck her. "When Cass is on the stand, can you ask her anything? Ask her something for me?"

"What did you have in mind?" Mr. Baldacci answered the question with a question. He put his elbow on the table and the adjoining fist to his mouth. He raised his eyebrows.

"We had an unfortunate incident happen at our house last month," Josie said, picking her words carefully. "Someone threw a rock through the window in our sitting room. The old glass broke off in a solid chunk and acted like a guillotine. It decapitated my grandmother's best friend." Josie choked at that point and couldn't finish. The loss of such a beautiful life was too tragic to talk about.

"We want to know if she hired someone to throw the rock," P.J. came to Josie's rescue. "Can you ask her about that? She'd be under oath . . ."

"Unless we can connect the breaking of the window with this murder trial," Mr. Baldacci shook his head slowly, "I won't be able to bring that up. Besides, it will be difficult to prove she had anything to do with that since she was locked up, and being under oath doesn't guarantee Coven would tell the truth. People often lie under oath when faced with a murder charge. Now, let's continue going over your testimony.

"Josie, how long had you known Cass?"

"I met her when I started work at Sanderson & Sons, right after graduating college. That was just over a year ago."

"What kind of relationship did you have with her?"

"It was good, most of the time, until I suspected her of stealing my material."

"What did you do then?"

"I just took security measures so she couldn't do that anymore."

"What type of 'measures'?"

"Like when I worked at home, I would save it to a disk and bring it to work with me instead of emailing it like I used to. I also stopped leaving work lie on my desk whenever I left the office or even just went to the ladies' room."

"How did she react to that?"

"She started to get frustrated; but, didn't seem to suspect anything."

"Why did you leave town?"

"Someone attacked me at knifepoint one night when Cass chose me to work late and to take out the garbage after work."

"What do you mean, you were 'chosen'?"

"Normally, Cass took the garbage out, but she had to go out of town for an afternoon appointment. Because it was stormy, she sent everyone else home and told me she to take out the trash. It got dark by 5 p.m. So, when I took the trash out, I couldn't see much. Someone sneaked up behind me and held a knife to my throat. A raspy voice told me to leave town or I would be sorry. I was scared for my life; so, I listened."

"Did you report the incident to the police?"

"Yes, but I didn't feel that would stop the threat from being carried out."

"When did the two of you meet?" Baldacci turned his attention to P.J.

"We met when Josie moved to New York City and started working at my mom's office. Josie rented the loft above our garage."

"Did you know Cass at that time?"

"No. I never officially met her. I saw her for the first time when I came to Lakewood to tell Josie I wanted to date her. My first contact with Cass was tackling her to keep her from shooting Josie."

"Did you know it was Cass? Had Miss Buchannon ever told you she was involved with the FBI in a sting operation to capture Coven?"

"No, it was nothing like that. After I found out that I jumped into the middle of it all, I just assumed Josie hadn't told me or my family about what was going on because she was under orders from the FBI not to disclose any information regarding their operation." Josie nodded in agreement.

"Besides, like P.J. said, well indirectly, we hadn't started dating, yet," Josie said.

"That's a lot of questions," P.J. said. "Wasn't any of that in your files?"

"Most of it was," Baldacci admitted. "But, I wanted to give you the 'third degree', as they call it, to give you a feeling of what it will be like on the witness stand. In fact, the defending attorney will be asking you some tough questions and some that will seem tainted, like, "Did you two collaborate on pushing Coven's buttons until she cracked?' or "Did you set Ms. Coven up to take the fall for threatening you because you were trying to get revenge for her allegedly stealing your work?"

"No, no! None of that happened!" Josie was offended. "I don't work that way. I just wanted to get credit for my own work, not let someone steal my ideas."

"Of course, not," Baldacci said. "But, you can't let the defense attorney get under your skin. You have to answer the questions truthfully, calmly and without outbursts that could lead the judge to think you may be hiding something."

"I've seen that happen on TV lawyer shows," P.J. said. "I thought it was all scripted. Huh!"

"Where do you think writers get their material? From real court cases, of course," Baldacci said. He went on to ask a couple more tough questions before giving them a couple of tips on what to do if they got stuck. If they froze, they were to look at him for a nod or an objection. He promised them he would do his best to keep the defense attorney from railroading them. Then he sent them home.

"Why don't you stay the night, P.J.? I can't think straight anymore; and, I don't want to be alone. Here are the keys. You drive. I'll drop you off at work tomorrow." P.J. took the keys and drove them to his apartment first to pick up an overnight bag, then on to the Victorian Drama style home where Eleanor had a hamburger-tomato hotdish ready and waiting for them.

Over supper, the three came up with the idea to offer a monetary reward for information leading to the arrest and conviction of the person or persons who threw the stone into their window causing the death of Eleanor's best friend.

The three took their dessert into the family room and turned on the television. Josie purposely channel surfed until she found a rerun of Three's Company hoping to use laughter to quell the uneasy feeling she brought home with her. She curled up on the couch with P.J. while Eleanor picked up her cross stich project. When the comedy was over, Eleanor suggested a game of Rummy. The young couple agreed; and, Josie got the playing cards out while Eleanor made some hot chocolate and popcorn. They played until 11 p.m. when they decided it was time to call it a night.

Waking in P.J.'s arms on the couch was becoming a bad habit, Josie thought the next morning when it happened again. She shifted her shoulder, which was enough to tell her she had a crick in her neck. *I may need a chiropractor appointment,* she thought. Her eyes popped open as she was reminded that she and P.J. had a counseling session with the minister after work today. She sprang up from the couch with such force it woke her slumbering groom-to-be.

"What's up?" he asked. "Besides you, that is?" He rubbed his eyes and looked at her again. Josie grabbed a throw pillow from the floor and threatened to bean him with it.

"You Smart Alec, you!" Josie shouted! "How can you be so clever so early in the morning?"

"You know me," he teased, then sat up, running his fingers through his hair. "Seriously, what made you launch yourself off the couch?"

"I just remembered we need to go see Rev. Van Meveren after work tonight. We'd better take turns showering and get on with the day."

Just then Eleanor walked into the family room; the smell of bacon following her in.

"I was wondering when you two were going to get up. Don't you set the alarm on your cellphone when you sleep down here? Breakfast is almost ready. Josie, why don't you go shower first, come down for breakfast before putting on your make-up. You can finish getting ready after breakfast while P.J. showers."

"Great idea, Grams! Thanks!"

"I am getting hungry," P.J. said. "I don't think I could wait to eat until after she got her makeup on." Whop! Josie hit him with the pillow she had been holding.

Showers and breakfast went smoothly, thanks to Eleanor's suggestion. The couple decided that would be a good order in which to conduct morning ablutions once they were wed and living together. On the way to work though, P.J. said, "You know, I've heard that couples can save water by showering together . . ."

"That wouldn't work with us in the morning," Josie said.

"Why not?" P.J. demanded.

"Because, silly! We wouldn't just be washing each other's backs, and you know it!"

P.J. found that so funny he laughed every time he thought about it throughout the day. Josie blushed, herself, whenever it crossed her mind. And, because they were so preoccupied with dreams of how married life would be, the day flew right by. Soon, P.J. was picking Josie up at her home where she dropped off her car, and they were on the way to the church.

Rev. Van Meveren sat at his desk with the door open. Josie still rapped on the door just to be polite.

"Come in!" The Reverend invited. "Have a seat." He motioned to two barrel-shaped chairs facing his desk. Josie slid through and into the far chair, leaving the closer one to P.J. She popped up once to smooth her maroon skirt. She had purposely worn the longer suit and black pantyhose with flat dress shoes to give a more demure appearance. The pink shell that coordinated with the suit had a high jewel neckline. Jose felt no need to flash any cleavage, not that any of her tops did that, but she didn't want to take any chances.

"My, don't you look nice today, Josie," The Reverend said, as if he was reading her mind.

"Thank you, Rev. Van Meveren," she said, stifling a giggle at the way his name rhymed. P.J. reached over and clapped his hand on her shoulder, also seeming to read her mind.

"How are you today, P.J.? Is it all right if I call you P.J.?" the Reverend asked.

"Of course," P.J. answered, reaching over the desk to shake hands with the minister. "I'm fine. How are you?"

"Good, good. So, you've set the date for your wedding. That would be the first Saturday in April, correct?" The young couple nodded in unison. "P.J., I see you were baptized and confirmed at a sister church in New York City. Will you be transferring here once you're married?"

"Yes, sir! In fact, I'm prepared to do that now, if you like,"

"That won't be necessary. It's been my experience that it can get messy if the wedding doesn't go off as planned. In the meantime, you are welcome to take communion here.

"Moving on to the marriage ceremony, who will be your maid of honor and best man? They will be signing the marriage certificate."

"Vikki, that is Victoria Dale," Josie answered.

"And, Stanley Baker," P.J. provided.

"What time of day were you interested in starting the ceremony? Keep in mind it can take anywhere from 30 minutes to an hour, depending on how many activities you want to incorporate into the service."

He kept asking questions, which Josie fielded with ease. P.J. wasn't quite as forthcoming with answers, deferring to his bride-to-be, since all that business was usually "the woman's domain." By the time the Reverend was through with them, P.J. had started to sweat. He was used to the younger ministers in his home church. They liked to talk sports and joke around a little bit to keep the atmosphere light. This guy was older and straight as an arrow, by the book. P.J. was sitting on the edge of his seat by the time the Reverend dismissed them.

"One word of advice before you leave," Rev. Van Meveren said, as the couple stood. "'Never let the sun go down on your anger.' That's from the Bible, of course; and, truer words were never spoken. You would do well to heed them."

"Yes, sir, we will!" Josie and P.J. both said and made their escape.

The next day Josie decided to call Special Agent Freeman to see what news he had for her.

"I've been out to visit with that Coven woman," he said. "She's a tough cookie. Maybe a little crazy, too. When I asked her if she knew anybody on the outside that would throw a rock through your window, she just laughed. She never did answer. On the other hand, your honorable mayor isn't so honorable. He and his wife copped to many things, but hiring thugs wasn't on the list. Geez, you'd think I was their priest, the way they confessed to sins like hate, greed, jealousy; all of which could make a good motive; but, they kept saying they never acted on any of it. The missus, in particular, kept saying she was a 'woman of God' and wouldn't stoop that low. Mayor Glass just got indignant after a bit and threatened to lawyer up. I told them not to leave town."

Josie hung up the phone more disappointed that when she first dialed. Even the FBI was striking out. She hoped the reward the paper would print this week would prove more useful. As she went back to work on a storyboard, Josie couldn't help but wonder what other roadblocks they would encounter. Just like a bad mystery movie, the phone rang with more foreboding news.

"Hi, Josie? Sid Silverstein, here," the familiar voice said.

"Oh, hi, Sid! What's up?" Josie asked, not really wanting to know. Sid usually called only when he had some paperwork for her; and, she wasn't really in the mood for that kind of business.

"Your grandmother told me you were getting married. So, I thought I'd take the opportunity to congratulate you on your engagement."

"Thanks, Sid."

"Also, you and I should meet so we can discuss the need for a prenuptial agreement." Sid paused to let what he had just said sink in. "I know you believe you're in love, and so is this Coleson guy. And, that's probably all true, but you have a responsibility to you late father to protect the estate he built and left you. Even the best-matched couples can become disillusioned after a couple of months or years and file for divorce. You want to protect yourself from losing up to half of your holdings to an ex-husband."

Josie sighed. She didn't want to think about this right now. She had a ton of work to do. All these meetings were putting her further and further behind. She took a deep breath and said, "Sid, I hear what you're saying. I really do; but, this is not the time to discuss this. I'm swamped with work. Can we do this in a month or two?"

"Sure thing, Josie. Just don't let it go too long. If you get too close to your wedding date, when was that again? Anyway, there is a specific amount of lead time needed to file the papers before the wedding. Just keep that in mind. I will call you again in four weeks. Please be prepared to at least set a meeting date, okay?"

"Yes, alright, Sid. I'll mark it on my calendar, okay?" Sid hung up with her promise. *Ooh!* Josie *thought. How am I going to break this to P.J.?*

Chapter Fourteen
Cass's Court Case

Argh! There were too many lawyers, cops, Special FBI Agents. Just too many officials were making Josie's life frustrating. She ran to the rest room, tore down a wad of paper towels and buried her face in them. She let out a bloodcurdling scream, at least it would have been if she hadn't stifled it. The only thing that came out was a whispered screech. With the bathroom door closed, no one else heard a thing. Josie took a deep breath and let it out heavily. Not only was Cass's court date tomorrow, but now she had to find a way to tell P.J. Sid wanted him to sign a prenup. Of course, there's always a chance that he would agree. Both his parents worked for big businesses, and would probably even approve of the action. Then even P.J's inheritance would be secure.

Josie returned to her desk making the decision to wait until she saw P.J. face to face before bringing up this legal matter. She might even put it off until after the first of the year. She wanted him to look into her eyes and know this was not her idea, nor did she want it to come between them.

The phone rang as soon as she had sat in her chair.
"Josie Buchannan here. How can I help you?"

"This is Prosecutor Tanner Louwagie from the District Attorney's office. I was hoping to stop by your office this afternoon to go over your testimony for the Cassandra Coven case going to court tomorrow. I apologize for the late notice, but I've been out of state on vacation. When I heard it had been moved up, I flew back early to take the case myself. Please say you can clear your schedule for this afternoon."

"Uh, sure. I should be able to do that between now and . . . when you arrive, which would be . . . ?"

"I'm just leaving Lakeside Technologies where I spent time with your fiancée, P.J. Coleson; so, unless I get lost, I should be there in just under ten minutes."

That settled that. It would be the icing on the legal cake. Josie got on the intercom to Vikki to ask her to help clear her schedule for the afternoon, and to be specific as to why. Josie didn't want to get the reputation that she cancelled appointments to run off and do fluffy personal stuff. *Like Cass did,* Josie thought, and remembered one more time how Cass took her shopping the day she earned her promotion.

By the time the prosecutor arrived, Josie was working on calmly sitting at her desk, thinking about her testimony. However, she jumped out of her skin when Vikki announced the arrival of Mr. Tanner Louwagie. Within seconds he came swaggering into her office, extending his hand in greeting. She shook it.

"Pleased to meet you in person, Ms. Buchannon," he beat her to the greeting. Swirling to check out the distance to the brown flowered couch, he backed up and took a seat without being asked.

"Same here," Josie said, keeping it as informal as possible. "Can I get you something to drink? Coffee, water?"

"No thanks. We have a lot to go over and not much time to spare. Please answer the following questions to the best of your ability." Without further ado, Mr. Louwagie launched into many of the same questions Special Agent Freeman had asked her at the police station. That was uncanny, Josie thought, since Freeman was actually working on Virginia's murder, not Lew's. He did add a couple of his own.

"Did you suspect Cass of committing the murder and why?"

"Over the time I worked for her, Cass kept pealing back layers of her personality. She kept getting more sinister and mean, sneaky, really. I suspected her of stealing my ideas, and I was able to prove it by hiding my work until staff meetings. But, I can't say I ever considered her to be any more of a safety risk. Not until I left town. That gave me time to think about everything that happened up until then. I didn't mention it to anyone, but I started having nightmares about the night I was attacked at knife point; and, in the dreams, I strongly smelled Cass's perfume and felt the contour of her body against my back during the attack. It's like sleep clarified my perception of the event and beefed up my senses."

"That is quite possible that's what happened," Louwagie said. "So, would you say you were predetermined to find Cass guilty of murder and maybe due to this Princess Plan you concocted, she, being a sensitive person, snapped. And, that's the only reason she took a potshot at you? That she may be innocent of Lew Sanderson's murder?"

"What? That's just ludicrous. Of course not. Cass admitted it to me when she pointed her gun at me. She told me about her plan to take over the company by inheriting it from Lew. It's all recorded on the video tape. Surely, you've seen the tape . . ."

"Yes, I did. This morning, before coming here. I'm sorry I had to ask you such an off-the-wall question. As you may know, I have to prepare you for being cross-examined by the attorney for the defense. She's going to be asking you all kinds of self-incriminating questions that you must answer calmly, truthfully, and without faltering. Any wavering on your part will not look good to the judge or the jury."

"Yes, I figured that's why you were doing it. I couldn't imagine why you thought I might lie about what happened, especially when the incident had been recorded." Josie tried to relax.

"That's right. Preparation is what we're going for here. I just want you to know I believe everything on that tape and whatever else you want to tell me. Like, did you have a grudge against Coven for not maintaining your friendship once you had to start protecting your work? Did the two of you start resenting each other anywhere along the line?"

"Well, I was hurt when she started doing all those mean things. I did think we were friends, but I had to admit to myself that I was in the wrong because I thought she, the manager, and I, the employee, could really be friends. No, I didn't hold a grudge for that; I felt sorry for her that she felt she had to steal someone else's ideas to stay on top."

"Okay, you pass the test. Just be ready for all kinds of outlandish accusations or hints on the part of the defense attorney. She'll be grasping for straws. If you think of anything else, here's my card. Call me. I will be up past midnight working on this. We could also meet at the court house prior to the start time if you want to go over anything else."

Josie hadn't thought of anything new between the time Mr. Louwagie left her office and when the judge's gavel fell, announcing that the case of The People vs. Cassandra

Coven case was in session. P.J. had picked up Josie at her home at 9:30 a.m. to drive to the courthouse together.

"Are you nervous, Josie?"

"Some," she admitted. "You?"

"No. The facts speak for themselves. Everything is on the video tape. I'm sure the jury won't take any time at all to deliberate and deliver a guilty verdict." With that, they entered the courthouse.

Josie was on the witness stand, doing her best not to catch Cass's eye. She kept her attention on Mr. Louwagie as he asked her for her side of the story between her and Cass. Then, she looked at the defense attorney's nose, lips, necklace, anything but her eyes as she asked questions much like Josie had been prepared for. Then came a line of questioning she hadn't been prepared for.

"Do you like Cassandra Coven?"

"I did. Back when we were working together and were having fun. My . . . enthusiasm for her . . . company . . . diminished as she showed her . . . dark side." Josie struggled with finding the right words to express her current change of heart. She looked over at Mr. Louwagie. He nodded, indicating she was doing a good job.

"And, now?" defense attorney Yvonne Dragger prompted firmly. Josie took a moment to glance over at Cass, who was fiddling with her fingernails, which were her own, not the fake ones she used to wear to work. She didn't even look up.

"Now, I would have to say, I feel sorry for her; but, I'm no longer on a friendship basis with her. I hope she gets the help she needs; but, beyond that, I . . . am . . . ready to move on." Josie nodded as if to punctuate her statement.

"So, you don't like her? You'd be happy if she got a life sentence or even the death penalty?"

"I didn't say that," Josie said calmly.

"But, you were thinking it?"

"Objection!" Mr. Louwagie stood to emphasize his point. "Leading the witness."

"Sustained," Judge Anderson ruled. "Ms. Dragger, if you are through with this witness, please do not stretch this out any longer. Right now, it is obvious you are just going for a mercy plea."

"I withdraw the question, Your Honor. I am through with this witness; but, I reserve the right to recall her, and to treat her like a hostile witness."

"You may recall her later, if need be. Mr. Louwagie, please call your next witness.'

"The prosecution calls Paul Coleson, Jr. to the stand." P.J. was sworn in, just as Josie had been, and was seated. Mr. Louwagie began asking the same questions he had asked during his interview with P.J. and getting the same answers as to how P.J. had rescued Josie from being shot by Cass. He had heard most of Cass's confession as he sneaked up on the office door that dreadful night, then lunged at Cass to change her trajectory and to subsequently disarm her. Josie noticed that P.J. was able to relay the incident with calm humility. He didn't use it to grandstand as a self-proclaimed hero. *Ah, but he is a hero to me*, she thought. She nearly swooned with the thought. *P.J. looks so handsome in that navy suit. Maybe I should have picked navy for our wedding color.*

Soon, Mr. Louwagie was finished; and, Ms. Dragger took over. She stood up, smoothing her black and white pin-striped skirt, and approached the witness box. She leaned in close and gazed into P.J.'s eyes.

"How well did you know Cass before you disarmed her that night?" she asked softly, purposely using the same word P.J. had. P.J. looked at her calmly, leaning back in his chair ever so slightly.

"I had never met the woman before that night. In fact, we've never even spoken to each other," he said calmly.

"I suppose, though, that Ms. Buchannon had confided in you what had been transpiring at her office prior to the date in question, had she not?" The defense attorney continued to maintain eye contact with the witness.

"Actually, no," P.J. said confidently. "I barely knew Josie at the time. I had been out in the field on my job training for college while all that was going on. I didn't hear about it until later."

"Oh," was the disappointed response from the defense attorney as she turned away. "I have no more questions for this witness."

"The people submit this surveillance disk as Exhibit C," Mr. Louwagie said. Earlier he had submitted the prescription bottle with Cass's fingerprints on (found in a nearby trashcan) and the Colt 45 and accompanying bullets Cass used as the attempted murder weapon on Josie as Exhibits A and B.

"Bailiff, please take People's Exhibit C and play it on that DVD player," the judge ordered. The sleeve of his robe fluttered as he co-directed with his hand. The muscular bailiff accommodated the order. Soon, the entire assembly was watching as the frightful scene was replayed on the television screen. Josie's pulse pounded as she relived the heart-stopping event. P.J. squeezed her hand as if he could feel her fright. It was reassuring to have him there beside her. Hopefully, they would all be putting this behind them soon. She still hadn't found the right time to talk to P.J. about Sid's request; and, she wasn't going to upset them both any more than they had been for today.

The video ended; and, the bailiff removed the compact disk from the player and placed it on the evidence table. The courtroom went abuzz with comments from the attendees.

"Well, we've all seen the video with Ms. Coven's confession on it, and the attempted murder of her second employer, Ms. Josie Buchannon," Judge Anderson said, regaining the attention of the courtroom. Addressing the jury, he said, "You, the jury, will be considering the fate of this woman, Cassandra Coven, based solely on the evidence. You will not consider any outbursts during the trial or any allocations by the defense attorney that have been deemed leading, badgering or seducing the witnesses." He went on to give them specific instructions on how to handle their verdict and then dismissed them from the courtroom. "This court is recessed until the jury has reached its decision. At the risk of sounding overconfident, I recommend you retire to the adjoining recess rooms as I don't believe this decision will require more than one hour. In other words, stick around."

Judge Anderson hit his gavel and left the room, as did the court reporter and the bailiff.

"Come with me," Mr. Louwagie told Josie and P.J. They followed him into a nearby room that appeared to be a conference room with a telephone. They took chairs around the table and looked at one another.

"This shouldn't take long, like Judge Anderson said," the lawyer said. "All the evidence is there. Any jury in their right mind will convict within seconds of entering their sequestered room."

"What happens next?" P.J. asked.

"When the verdict comes back, that phone will ring and ask us to return to the courtroom. At that time, the verdict will be read and the judge will pronounce sentence. Or, he may delay the sentencing for a time to be determined in order to give him more time to research similar cases for the appropriate judgment."

"Not unlike court cases I've seen on television," P.J. said, nodding. Josie kept quiet. She didn't want to put a hex on anything. She didn't want Cass to get off on a technicality. *Not that I hate her, but she did some very bad things,* Josie thought.

Suddenly, the telephone rang. Mr. Louwagie picked up the receiver and said hello. "Thank you." He returned the receiver to the cradle before speaking. "Just as I expected. The jury is back."

The three followed the crowd back into the courtroom. The aisle seemed longer than the one at church, but Josie followed Mr. Louwagie up to the row of seats behind the table at which the lawyer stood near his chair. The jury filed in and stood as well. The bailiff entered and reminded others to stand, with an "All rise. The honorable Judge George R. Anderson, presiding," and the judge entered.

Once again Judge Anderson banged his gavel and said, "Be seated." Looking to the jury, he asked, "Have you come to a verdict in the case of The People vs. Cassandra Coven in the Murder of Lewis Sanderson?"

"We have, your honor," the foreman said and handed a folded piece of paper to the bailiff, who gave it to the judge. Judge Anderson read it and returned it to the bailiff, who in turn, returned it to the foreman.

"What say you?" the judge asked.

"In the case of The People vs. Cassandra Coven in the Murder of Lewis Sanderson, the jury finds the defendant guilty in the first degree."

"The jury's verdict will be so recorded. Have you a verdict in the adjoined case of The People vs. Cassandra Coven in the Attempted Murder of Josephine Buchannon?"

"We have, your honor." The foreman gave another folded piece of paper to the bailiff, who in turn repeated the same process as with the first verdict. The judge read it and returned it.

"What say you?" he asked.

"In the adjoined case of The People vs. Cassandra Coven in the Attempted Murder of Josephine Buchannon, we find the defendant guilty as charged."

"This verdict will also be recorded. The jury is hereby dismissed with our gratitude for its service," Judge Anderson nodded and the members of the jury stood as one and left the courtroom without looking at the defendant.

"Cassandra Coven, please rise," the judge ordered. The defendant and her attorney both stood. *Cass looked good in county orange, Josie thought. Now, cut that out*, she chided herself. *This is serious.*

"Ms. Coven, your plea of 'Guilty with Extenuating Circumstances' was entered at the beginning of the case. I failed to note any extenuating circumstances. Since the foreman didn't mention it, either, it appears the jury didn't either. Do you have a statement to make before I pronounce sentence upon you?"

He's pronouncing sentence today! Josie thought. *Thank God, there will be no more suspense!*

There was a pregnant pause that had Josie wondering if Cass was simply refusing to speak. But, then, she turned around to face the gallery. She wet her lips before speaking.

"I can imagine you all thought I was going for the insanity plea. I probably should've. But, with my calm confession on the surveillance tape, you probably saw a cool, calm, and collected premeditated murderer. Actually, I did, too. I didn't realize I came off that way. I really was very upset finding out that everything I had worked for went to someone else. I risked a lot trying to pull off the plan I had with Lew. My first plan, that is. I wanted him to marry me and just GIVE me the company. I had to settle for being his mistress and hope I had been put in his will. I still say his death was an accident. I really didn't know he was allergic to Viagra. I was just tired of him setting me aside and sticking up for Josie with no good reason. It was terrible not getting his full attention. Anyway," she turned back toward the judge, "I would just ask the court for mercy. I don't know how long I can handle being in prison. Please be lenient."

Josie didn't think she heard an apology in there anywhere. She looked at P.J. who shook his head, seeming to think the same thing. She looked Out on the gallery and saw a lot of heads being shaken. Nobody seemed to believe Cass.

"I didn't hear a word of remorse in your monologue, Ms. Coven," the judge echoed everyone's thoughts. "Therefore, I have no choice but to sentence you to life without parole for the Sanderson murder and an additional 25 years for the attempted murder of Ms. Buchannon, to be served consecutively. Maybe you will have enough time to see the error of your ways. Furthermore, you may not initiate contact—in any way, shape, or form—with either Josephine or Eleanor Buchannon or P.J. Coleson. Doing so will immediately gain you solitary confinement at graduated levels for each offence." Judge Anderson let the gavel fall one more time and watched, along with the rest of the courtroom, as two State Patrol officers entered the room and led Cass away. It wasn't until she had left the room that Josie began to breathe again.

Josie turned to P.J. and they hugged each other. They could finally relax. The threat was being put away for life, and then some.

Chapter Fifteen

Hitting a Sour Note

With so many other meetings going on, Josie had all but forgotten that Roberta wanted to practice their Thanksgiving solo together a few times before the entire choir started working on it. Roberta actually called the office shortly after Sid had to remind Josie to stop by after work that very same day.

"Well, I won't be able to discuss Sid's proposal with P.J. tonight!" Josie said aloud. She gave up on the campaign she was working on, grabbed her gray trench coat and headed out the door. She needed time to think, and her brain had just shut down on work. She hopped in her car and headed to the park for some fresh air. Once she parked the car, she locked her purse in the trunk and put her keys in her coat pocket. It was a good thing she had worn her cranberry pantsuit and flat shoes, since she automatically headed down the walking path at a good clip. She was halfway around the duck pond before she realized she had gone further than she had planned. Oh, but it felt good to wear off some of the tension that had started building ever since she saw the newspaper article about Cass's trial date being set. Then Sid had to add to the pressure with this nonsense about a prenuptial agreement. Josie had only heard about those papers on television shows. She didn't know anyone, personally, who had had one drawn up. With the way she felt about P.J., and how she knew he felt about her, she was certain their love—and their marriage—would last practically forever. And, if she died before he did, she would surely want him to have everything. Everything that is, except a small stipend to keep Grams in the lifestyle to which she had become accustomed.

Josie stopped along the trail and picked up a fist-size rock. She heaved it into the pond. It startled a family of mallards and caused ripples that extended back to the bank. Instantly, she regretted having caused the creatures any fright. In her distraction, she could have hit one and even killed it. *I can't believe I did that, acting irrationally, strictly out of frustration,* she thought. Then she continued her way around the pond, retrieved her purse from the trunk of her car and headed over to the Bates' house to rehearse with Roberta.

"I see you decided to show up." Roberta greeted her at the door. They eyed each other before Roberta held the door open for Josie.

"Of course," Josie said. "I never said I wouldn't."

"The piano is in the family room through this door," Roberta said, and led the way. She picked up her music folder off the piano and pulled out their duet. She sat at the piano and ran through the introduction, switching to playing just their parts when they got to their entrance. It was apparent she had warmed up before Josie arrived. Josie sang softly until her voice warmed up. The rest of her had warmed up by then as well, so she slid out of her trench coat. On the second run through, she followed the dynamics of the piece and worked on harmonizing with Roberta.

"Not bad," Roberta said when she had finished the piano coda at the end of the second go-round. "A couple more rehearsals and you should have it down well enough."

Josie felt she had done better than Roberta was saying, but she knew by now that was about as good as she was going to get out of her duet partner.

"I'm sorry, Roberta. I will have it down cold next time. As I said, I've been otherwise occupied lately. When would you like to get together again?" Josie asked, working on staying unprovoked.

"Why don't we plan to stay late after choir next week? That way, you'll already be warmed up." Roberta said, patronizing Josie. "I'll walk you to the door." Josie grabbed her trench coat and nearly trotted to the front door. It was obvious Roberta didn't want to visit, to get to know each other better, or anything along friendly lines. Far be it for Josie to overstay her welcome.

"Goodbye!" Roberta said as Josie crossed the threshold, and closed the door on her heels. Josie glanced back out of surprise and noticed the hall lights went out. Josie turned back to the sidewalk and headed toward her car.

Suddenly, the Bates' sprinkler system went on, drenching Josie with icy cold water. She gasped and scooted back to the door. She knocked, but no one came to the door. Glancing at the dark windows, she thought she saw the curtains move ever so slightly, but still no one came to the door. *Roberta must have gone upstairs*, Josie thought, giving the rude woman the benefit of the doubt. *I'll just have to rush through the sprinkler and go home*. Josie pulled on her coat in an attempt to stay dry, screwed up her resolve, and sprinted down the sidewalk. Once near the driver's door of her car she got in. By then, even her coat was soaked. She cranked the heat up because being wet on a cold October night was chilling. Her teeth started to chatter with cold.

By the time Josie reached her own home, she had started sneezing. She rushed into the house and draped her coat over a kitchen chair to let it dry.

"Achoo!" Josie sneezed again.

"What's this?" Eleanor asked, entering the kitchen. "I heard you sneezing all the way down the hall. Look at you! You're soaking wet? Whatever happened?" Grams reached for the hand towel hanging on the oven handle and gave it to Josie, who wiped her face with it. Water had trickled down from her dripping hair.

"I don't know for sure; but, I think Roberta turned her sprinkler system on as I left on purpose." Josie wiped her arms and then her legs. "I have to get out of these wet clothes."

"You do that, dear, and come back down for some hot tea." Eleanor said as she guided Josie toward the back stairs, then turned toward the stove to fill the tea kettle. By the time Josie returned, clad in her pajamas and winter bathrobe and slippers, Eleanor had tea ready. "This is Echinacea tea. It will help ward off a cold. Or, if you already have one, it will help ease the symptoms."

"You really do believe in natural cures, don't you, Grams?" Josie blew on the new brew to cool it off.

"Of course, pussycat," Eleanor replied. "Why put unnecessary drugs into your body. Herbs are more easily digested and have fewer side effects. They're not perfect, by any means, but certainly worth trying. Now, tell me again, what happened?"

Josie shook her head and took a deep breath before speaking. "I left work early because Sid Silverstein called and talked to me about getting P.J. to sign a prenuptial agreement. I couldn't think about work anymore, so I went for a walk in the park before going over to Roberta's to practice. She met me at the door and was a bit short with me. She took me to the family room where she played the piano, and we worked on our duet. We agreed to practice again after choir next week. Then she gave me the bum's rush and her sprinklers hosed me down on the way down the sidewalk. I went back to the house and knocked on the door to see if she could shut it off, but the lights were out. I thought maybe I'd seen the curtain move a little, but I can't be sure. You know it's been getting darker earlier and earlier. And, being all wet, it could have been water drops running down the side of my face."

"At least, you've stopped sneezing," Eleanor pointed out. She smiled warmly at her granddaughter. Josie couldn't help but smile back.

"Yeah, but my throat's starting to feel scratchy. I'd better get to bed." She took a couple of gulps of the cooled tea and dumped the rest in the sink. Then she stepped over to give her grandmother a hug and a goodnight kiss. "Thanks, Grams! Nobody takes care of me like you do!"

"Goodnight, dear," Eleanor hugged her back and released her. "I'll be up shortly. I just want to rinse out the tea cups. If you feel worse in the morning, let me know. I can always whip up an old-fashioned mustard plaster."

Josie smiled, nodded, and headed off to bed.

Chapter Sixteen
Arresting Suspects

The next morning, Josie was coughing up phlegm and looking for that mustard plaster.

"You had better call in sick to work," Eleanor advised as she tucked Josie in on the couch.

"I can barely whisper. You'd better be right next to me to help!" Eleanor nodded and went to get the telephone. Josie dialed and whispered to Vikki her dilemma. As Josie had anticipated, Vikki was not able to understand her, so she handed the transceiver to her grandmother.

"Hello, Vikki? This is Eleanor Buchannon (pause). Yes, Josie's grandmother (pause). Yes, that was Josie trying to tell you she won't be in to work today because she has caught a nasty cold." Eleanor listened a bit more and said, "Of course, I'll tell her. Thank you, Vikki. Goodbye." As she hung up, Eleanor relayed Vikki's message. "She has to tell you not to leave the couch, except to go to the bathroom, and to drink all the tea I make for you. Sweet girl!"

Before Eleanor could return the cordless telephone to it's base in the kitchen, it rang. Pushing the send button, Eleanor answered it. She listened for a while and said, "Josie is in bed with a bad cold. She will have to call you on Monday as she has laryngitis as well. (pause) I will relay the message. Thank you, Special Agent Freeman. Goodbye."

Eleanor looked at Josie who was giving her the questioning stare.

"Special Agent Freeman said to tell you he has possession of a surveillance tape from Lakewood Technologies. It implicates a plant worker in the incident where P.J. burned his hands because the same young man was caught on film yesterday trying to get into P.J.'s car to plant some incriminating evidence. When he couldn't get in, he apparently keyed the supervisors car, wiped off the key and dropped it on P.J.'s desk. Luckily, another office worker saw him do it and reported it to the supervisor, who put two and two together once he left work yesterday and discovered the damage to his car. Special Agent Freeman said they made the arrest this morning and will be interrogating the suspect in just a few minutes."

"Hope they throw the book at him for what he's been doing to P.J.!" Josie said, in a stage whisper, which amounted to shouting in her condition. Then her hand flew to her throat and she winced.

"Bad move," she whispered softly. Eleanor ran to the bathroom and brought back some sore throat drops and pain reliever. She gave two pain reliever and one lozenge to Josie along with a glass of water.

"Take these and I'll make more Echinacea tea for you. Then you'd better get some rest," Eleanor said. Then she left for the kitchen. Josie stayed on the couch until Monday, following Vikki's and her grandmother's instructions to the letter. She had Eleanor call P.J., too, and ask him to stay away until next week, so he didn't catch her cold.

Late in the afternoon on Monday, Josie was feeling better. Her throat didn't hurt so much anymore; so, she called the police station and asked for Special Agent Freeman. She was told he had left for the state penitentiary; did she want to speak to Officer Rodriguez? Josie said, yes.

115

"Officer Rodriguez here," Josie heard. "How can I help you?"

"It's Josie Buchannon, returning Special Agent Freeman's call from Friday. Can you tell me about the man he arrested? The one from Lakewood Technologies. Did he confess to all the pranks that went on?"

"Yes, and more," the officer said, "but, I'm not allowed to disclose anymore. Just know that the young man is behind bars and will face trial because of what he did to your fiancé. He also said he hadn't been working alone. As for the rest, we'll have to see how that pans out."

"Wow! That's some break in both cases, then! Great!" Josie winced as her enthusiastic outburst scratched her throat.

"Yes, it is. Well, we will keep you posted as the case progresses. We've contacted Mr. Coleson, too, to let him know his prankster has been found. You have a great week, now." They said their goodbyes; and, Josie hurriedly dialed P.J. to celebrate the good news with him.

"What do you suppose Officer Rodriguez meant by 'he hadn't been working alone'?" Josie asked P.J. after she had relayed her conversation with the officer. "And, what connection is there for him to have been pulling pranks at work to having thrown a rock through our window?"

"Well, what if he had been hired by someone like the mayor or even Cass? What if one or the other had been jealous enough to hire him to create problems for you? You would be the connection. Cass would be out for revenge. The mayor would be in it for your house. They both had motive. And, Cass, at least, has a history to prove she is capable of murdering someone to get her way."

"You know, when I called the police station, the desk sergeant did say that Special Agent Freeman was out to the penitentiary. Do you suppose that means he is interrogating Cass again?"

"What I think is that the desk sergeant let slip something she shouldn't have," P.J. said. "But, it will certainly be interesting to find out if you're right!"

Chapter Seventeen
Concerts and Christmas Crimes

After talking so much on Monday, Josie had a relapse. Her laryngitis lasted the rest of the week causing her to have Eleanor call Annie to give Josie's regrets about having to miss choir practice. Josie could picture the arrogant smile on Roberta's face when she heard the news. She was probably going to speak with Annie about doing a solo instead of a duet even though Christmas was still six weeks away.

Josie hopped on the internet and emailed Vikki that she wouldn't be coming to work, either. She had everything she needed to work up some sketches at home. It wouldn't work to go into work because clients would be calling, expecting to actually talk to her, as would her employees. Vikki would keep them all at bay and relay any messages via email, per Josie's request. She didn't want to be tempted to talk too much if Vikki would call to relay messages. Even so, Josie had to be firm with Vikki on the matter, writing her with bold, capital letters: ***DO NOT CALL FOR ANY REASON, EXCEPT A FIRE!***

Soon, she was working hard on her laptop, using PowerPoint to put together ideas that had kept her awake the night before. *I should have gotten up, right then and there, and worked on them*, she thought. She kept plugging away until she found herself in the middle of her fourth presentation. She glanced at the ceiling and thumped her chin with her thumb as she contemplated the nuances of a specific scene she was trying to set.

"Time for lunch!" Eleanor called from the kitchen. Josie saved the document she was working on, threw back the afghan from her lap and padded down the hall. She pulled the sweater closed over her pajama top and pushed open the swinging door on the kitchen with her elbow.

"Mmmm. What smells so good, Grams?" Josie whispered.

"It's homemade chicken and dumpling soup. I know it's one of your favorites," Eleanor answered. "And, even though it's chicken noodle soup that gets credit for helping cure the common cold, dumplings are very similar." She set down a china bowl filled to the brim with the steaming concoction. Josie sat on the chair in front of it and sniffed at the steam, her eyes closed and a smile on her face. Eleanor put down her own bowl on the vacant space near her own chair and sat down. The two women bowed their heads while Eleanor said grace. "Come, LORD Jesus, be our guest. Let these gifts to us be blessed." They both said Amen and picked up their soup spoons.

Josie notice for the millionth time that the china bowls and spoons were family heirlooms. Granted, Grams usually brought them out for just special occasions. Somehow, Josie didn't count her being sick as a "special occasion".

"Grams, why the good china?" she whispered. "It's not a holiday."

"No, it's not, dear," Eleanor said. "However, I was watching an old episode of Little House on the Prairie. Charles was moonlighting to buy a set of china for Caroline. When he finally delivered it home, she set the table with it on an ordinary day. Laura asked her why she did that. Caroline answered that having her family all together for a meal made it a special day, not just an ordinary day. When I think of the close calls you've had this year, I can't imagine putting things off anymore."

Their conversation turned toward the holidays. Should they invite the Colesons up for Thanksgiving or Christmas or both? Or, maybe split the holidays?

"P.J. said his family would like to hear me sing my solos," Josie whispered between slurps of soup.

"That settles it! We have plenty of bedrooms. If they want to come up for Christmas, they wouldn't have to worry about getting stranded at the motel in inclement weather," Eleanor suggested. Josie thought of the tiny roadside inn with outdoor entry to the ten rooms. It was considered a bed and breakfast by the townspeople, but she felt that by big city standards it left a lot to be desired.

"I will invite them later this week when my voice comes back," she just managed to get out

They finished lunch in relative silence. Then Eleanor stood and picked up both soup bowls, saying, "You go to the couch and take a nap. 'Do not pass Go', do not open your laptop. Nothing. Go rest. I will do the dishes."

"Yes, Ma'am!" Josie whispered so strongly, it came out more like a bark. It triggered a coughing session. Josie had to take a drink of her milk to quiet the attack. "Mmnnh. Sorry!" ***That one hurt!*** She thought as she trotted out through the door and down the hall.

"And, no running!" Eleanor's voice came through the swinging door. It had a happy twinge to it, so Josie knew her grandmother wasn't angry with her.

Josie flopped onto the couch, pulled up the red, orange, green and brown afghan, and reached for the TV remote. She turned on her favorite television program before picking up her laptop, she nearly opened it before remembering Grams had told her not to do that. She gently set it back on the floor and closed her eyes while she listened to her program. Soon she had drifted off and was dreaming about her wedding day. The church was decorated with icy green and white satin ribbons. The bridesmaids all wore spring green dresses with bouquets of daisies and baby's breath. They were all up front by the minister and the groomsmen already. The organist was switching music, so there was a brief pause before she started playing the Bridal March. Josie looked down at her bouquet and noted she was carrying the traditional red roses with baby's breath. The music started and she glanced up at the man who stood by, ready to escort her down the aisle. Only the person in the beige tux next to her didn't have a face. Normally the father of the bride would be giving her away on her wedding day, but since her real father had been murdered before she found out who he was, Josie had started picturing Mr. Garvey in that role. She woke with a start, realizing she hadn't asked him, yet. She had better call him before his calendar fills up. Josie made a note on her laptop and went back to sleep; secure in the knowledge that she would fill that role tomorrow.

After a boring rest of the week, and a short visit from P.J. on Saturday, Josie was more than ready to go back to work on Monday. Luckily, so was her voice. Following her grandmother's instructions on rest, not talking, and drinking lots of herbal tea, her voice had returned. And, by Wednesday, she was delighted to get back to choir rehearsals as well.

"Alright!" Annie exclaimed, clapping her hands together, when Josie walked into the choir room. "It's great to have you back!" Annie was wearing her usual all-black ensemble with a black cardigan over the black shell. "I don't suppose you've had time to work on your Christmas solos, hmm?"

"Not really. Laryngitis is funny that way!" They both laughed at that. "However, I did get in one good rehearsal session with Roberta before I caught that cold. I'm confident we'll do well in two weeks when we've gotten a couple more practices in. In fact, we've planned to stay after choir tonight and next week to work on it here, if that's okay."

"Why, certainly! Just lock up when you leave. If you go out the other side door, you can lock it without a key." Annie nodded and stepped toward the piano which was Josie's cue that choir practice was about to start, and that she'd better take her seat.

Practice with Roberta later didn't go quite as badly as Josie had envisioned. Roberta was still cold, but went through the motions of getting down to work. Josie did her best to make the other woman feel appreciated. She complimented Roberta's fashionable fall outfit, thanked her for doing such a good job on the piano while accompanying them and even offered her a ride home if she needed one. She also never missed an opportunity to give Roberta a friendly smile. Grams always said, "If you see a person without a smile, give them one of yours." Of course, Josie knew that wasn't an Eleanor Original, but it certainly fit the situation.

"I brought my own car," Roberta said, giving Josie a furrowed brow. "I'll get home just fine. Thank you for offering."

"Okay. So, we'll do this again next Wednesday; and, we'll be ready for our duet on Thursday, Thanksgiving Day. Right?" Josie said with another smile, nodding her head.

"Yes. I think it will work out well." Roberta replied. And, forgetting herself for a moment, she added, "Did you hear about the pieces Annie gave me for New Year's Eve?"

"Not yet. What are they?" Josie asked, excited to have Roberta share anything with her besides "cold shoulder and hot tongue".

"This first one is just an anthem right out of the hymnal, which is easy schmeezy. You probably recognize it, right?"

"Right, but I'm sure it will sound beautiful when you do it. So, what's the other one?"

"This . . ." Roberta said, pulling a solo piece from her folder and spread it out on the piano to play for Josie. She began to sing, *"May God bless you with a bright New Year . . ."*

Josie kept silent, following along with the music, which lilted and flowed. *I probably would never have considered this piece, but it's pretty,* she thought, and said so when Roberta had finished. The two walked out of the church on a more comfortable note than ever before. Josie was beginning to look forward to performing her duet with Roberta next week.

Thanksgiving came and Josie and Roberta's duet went off without a hitch. After the service, the two received many compliments on how well they had done and how smoothly their voices blended. One elderly woman even asked them if they planned to do more duets throughout the coming year. Josie was surprised when Roberta said that was a likely possibility!

With the service being at 9 o'clock in the morning, P.J. was able to drive Josie and Eleanor down to New York City for Thanksgiving Dinner with his family. The big house came alive with the twins, Patty and Pauline, making a huge fuss over their soon-to-be sister-in-law.

"We missed you sooooo much!" they chimed and gave her a big group hug. With sweaters meshing and cheeks smacking with kisses, all three fell upon the living room couch. It was the beginning of a fun-filled family day with all the Thanksgiving trimmings.

When evening approached, the visiting trio headed back upstate to Lakewood. With heavy, nostalgic sighs, they settled back into their workday routines with Josie enjoying the added dimension of preparing for her Christmas solos.

< * >

The week before Christmas brought the first heavy ice storm of the season. The State Patrol issued a warning that no one should be on the roads for the remainder of the storm, plus allowing time for the county and city plows to sand the slick streets before returning to regular traffic. Josie called her staff and told them to take two days off. If she needed them, she would email their assignments; and, they could work from home. Vikki groaned because she didn't want to miss doing lunch with the bride-to-be. Hildy also groaned, but about all the work she imagined would pile up for her when she did return.

"Yahooooo!" Jessica shouted into the receiver causing Josie to wince in pain. "That means I can stay in bed with my new hubby! Thanks, Josie!" She hung up on Josie in her rush to be with her man.

"Well, I didn't expect THAT much excitement," Josie said to herself as she rubbed her ear with her finger. Then she went to work, calling her clients from home, to reschedule the day's meetings. In some cases, they were able to make some decisions over the phone, which gave Josie the green light to construct their ads that afternoon, even though she was stuck at home. Josie was relieved that her own workload wouldn't be as backed up as Hildy thought hers would be.

Late in the afternoon, P.J. called to say he had made it home from work.

"It took me nearly 45 minutes to get home," he said, noting it normally took him ten minutes. "I was starting to get frustrated. I even considered getting out and walking, but the ice would have cut my hair for me!"

"I'm glad you're safe!" Josie said. "I don't know why you went to work in this weather any way! You stay put. As much as I'd like to see you, you had better just stay home where it's safe."

"Don't worry! I will. Oh, say! While I was gripping the steering wheel so hard, I was also listening to the news on the radio. Did you hear about the jewelry store robbery? The crooks must have taken advantage of the weather keeping the workers home."

"Yes, I heard. Grams was listening to the same broadcast. She told me about that and about another crime. Let's see what was it? Hmm. I was actually working on some ads this afternoon, so I didn't hear it; but, I think she said there was a fire at the gas station on the south side of town. Someone tried to rob the place; and, when the owner walked in, the crook lit a match and dropped it into the waste basket. The owner had no choice but to let the crook escape in order to save his shop." Josie shook her head in disgust. "What's this world coming to?"

"Living in this small town has made me forget that crimes like those take place in New York City on a daily basis; and, it doesn't have to be related to bad weather, or anything like that," P.J. said.

"Well, I hope that has Officer Rodriguez and her crew on the lookout for more such activity," Josie said. "I'd hate to think the weather can keep law enforcement from protecting us."

"Just be sure you double check your door locks and turn on your security system before you go to bed every night." P.J. said. "I don't want anything to happen to my future bride; at least, not before the honeymoon!"

"Oh, you!" Josie snorted said goodnight.

Over the course of the week, the roads finally cleared off and everyone was back at work by Friday. Since Christmas

Day was on Monday, Josie instructed her staff to pack up what they needed for next week's work. They could take it home to work on Saturday and also have it there in case another storm hit town during Christmas week.

"I've also arranged for you to access your work emails from home. You can use the same password. You just need to enter this code when you go online to our web site." She distributed a sheet of paper to each staff member. "Be sure to keep this in a safe place; and, don't write anything on this paper that would tie the code to our website. This is an extreme caution to all of you to help prevent industry theft. Please consider this a huge honor to be trusted with this information; and, guard it with your life!"

Because it had started snowing again by mid-afternoon, Josie sent the staff home an hour earlier than normal, instructing them to put in that hour after supper. And, so it went that Josie spent most of the weekend catching up on lost hours from earlier in the week. She poured over her laptop until Eleanor begged her to come to the kitchen to eat. Saturday night, came; and, so did P.J.

"Make her take a break, P.J.," Eleanor told him when she answered the door. "She's been at it ever since she got home yesterday." She pointed to the living room, then she left the two lovebirds to themselves and headed toward the kitchen.

"Come on," P.J. said and closed the laptop on Josie's fingers. She gave him a mock angry glare. He took her hands in his and drew her away from the table and over to the couch. "I rented this great movie from Red Box. It's a real chick flick—figured you'd like it. Now, just stay on the couch while I plug it in."

He returned to the couch and slid in under the afghan next to Josie. He put his arm around her. She lifted her face to his for a kiss.

"Thanks, P.J. I guess I really do need a break. My eyesight was getting fuzzy." She opened and closed her eyes to activate the tear ducts. The movie previews started; and, they snuggled in a little closer together.

"Oh, I hope you don't mind; but, I asked your grandmother to join us. She offered to make popcorn." P.J. said.

As if on cue, Eleanor came through the door with a huge tray. On it were popcorn bowls and three mugs with hot chocolate.

"Thanks, Eleanor! You're great!" P.J. said as he freed his arms to help her with the tray. She set it in his hands, then lifted one bowl and one mug and took them to the recliner, leaving the rest for him and Josie.

"You're very welcome, P.J. It was nice of you to invite me to join you. I could have watched TV in my room, you know. I'm sure you and Josie have some wedding plans you could be working on."

"Nonsense. It's Christmas weekend, and we should spend it with family doing fun things. Beside, my family will be here tomorrow and none of us will get any free time then." He picked up the remote and hit "Play".

Just as P.J. had predicted, the movie was a big hit with the two women. He would not admit that he enjoyed it more than he had expected, but then no macho man would.

P.J. was also right about his family arriving the next day and creating havoc with the normally serene atmosphere of the old Victorian home. His twin sisters had a blast helping pick out the Christmas tree and decorating it. Eleanor had made extra popcorn the night before and had the girls stringing it along with cranberries for a real Old-Fashioned tree garland. After an oyster stew supper, also a family tradition, everyone sat around the living room sharing favorite Christmas stories. At 10 o'clock, Josie showed Patty and Pauline to her room where they would be sleeping. She pulled out some bride's magazines and showed them some ideas she had for bridesmaid dresses.

"I was wondering what you two thought of these styles? Would you consider wearing one of these as my bridesmaids?" she asked them.

"Ooh! Really?" Pauline asked. "They're pretty!"

"Of course, we'll be your bridesmaids!" Patty shouted. Squealing, they paged through the publications and chatted animatedly for over an hour. Mrs. Coleson had to come up and suggest they get some sleep.

"After all, you wouldn't want to fall asleep during Josie's solo in church tomorrow, would you?" she asked. The girls shook their heads and clamored for their pajamas. Then Josie showed Mrs. Coleson to the guest room where Eleanor had already directed Mr. Coleson who had brought up their suitcases. After saying goodnight, Josie went back down to the living room where P.J. had pulled out the hide-a-bed and made it. Josie would be bunking with Eleanor tonight, and P.J., on the hide-a-bed, but Josie wanted a goodnight kiss. P.J. didn't need any persuasion and met her in the center of the room. He took her in his arms and covered her mouth with his. Passion flowed deeply between the two. Josie was lost in the love he was showing her. His lips were full and hard on her soft mouth. His tongue pressed through to explore her mouth. Their tongues danced in harmony with the beating of her heart. Her pulse raced. Chills went up her spine; and, her knees went week. P.J.'s strong arms held her tightly to him. Her arms snaked around his neck. Their bodies pressed hard against each other, sending fiery signals throughout their lower regions. Josie gasped.

"You okay?" P.J. murmured in her ear. He kissed her hair, her ear, her neck.

"Mmmhmm," Josie purred back. "I love you."

"I love you, too," P.J. whispered in her other ear, then nibbled on it. Josie's body perked up and seemingly of its own will pressed harder against P.J.s. Then, suddenly, he pushed her away. "You had better go up to bed. Eleanor will be wondering where you are. Besides, I don't think I can take any more of this."

Josie took a deep breath and nodded in agreement. She didn't even trust her voice at this point. She just blew him a kiss and drifted toward the door. *The closer we get to our wedding day, the stronger my feelings are for him*, she thought. *I can tell he must be feeling the same way. We just have to hold out a little longer.*

Between P.J.'s hot kisses and her solo looming overhead, Josie drifted in and out of sleep the entire night. The dark circles under her eyes had Eleanor interrogating her the next morning.

"Merry Christmas, Josie! Oh! Didn't you sleep well? Did you sneak back down and spend more time with P.J. last night? What's going on? Aren't you feeling well?"

"I'm fine, Grams; just didn't sleep well. After all, I wasn't in my own bed; and, I have these solos today." She headed down to the bathroom on the main floor and stood in line. Apparently, P.J. had awakened early and decided to shower first. Eleanor headed to the kitchen to start breakfast. Cooking for six would take more time than for two. Soon, she had the whole house smelling like coffee and bacon.

"It's a mad house every morning before work," Mrs. Coleson told Eleanor as she helped prepare breakfast. She was still in her sky blue satin nightgown and bathrobe. "I normally get up before the girls. You know teenagers. They take their time with their makeup and hair. The twins are no different; they just take twice as long. My husband goes downstairs to shower, and I just beat them all to the bathroom. That way I'm ready for work before I make breakfast."

"I know what you mean. Luckily for Josie, I'm retired and don't need to fight over the shower with her," Eleanor said, and pointed to the cupboard where the dishes were kept. Mrs. Coleson took the cue and set the table. Josie and P.J. had pulled the table out after the movie Saturday night and put in the extra leaf. Everyone could sit at the kitchen table for breakfast. Christmas dinner, which Eleanor already had in the oven, would be served on the dining room table later.

Soon everyone crowded around the kitchen table and enjoyed Eleanor's cooking before heading off to church.

Josie left the family at the front door as she headed down to the choir room. They would find a pew in which to sit while she pulled her choir robe out of the closet and slid into it. *It's a shame we have to wear these,* she thought. *I spent a lot of money on this new dress.* She had fallen in love with it when she saw it in the bride's magazine. The magazine indicated the gown was for a personal attendant, but being evergreen, Josie figured it would work well for Christmas, so she ordered it. The slim satin skirt and fitted bodice really showed off her figure. P.J.'s appreciation of it gleamed in his eyes the moment he saw her in it that morning. Josie's mind was still on the sight when Annie called the choir to attention for warm-ups. Sixteen royal blue satin robes with yellow gold stoles turned to face her.

"Let's do a few deep breathing exercises, then we'll go through the numbers in the order in which they appear in the bulletin." Annie said, then lifted her baton and gave the pickup beat. She counted to ten as choir members breathed in through their noses being sure to draw it in with their diaphragms and not by lifting their shoulders.

Annie counted to ten again as they held their breaths, and a third time as they exhaled on a hiss. Vocal scales followed the breathing exercise.

"Open your folders and we'll begin. Josie, be ready to come in with your solos when it's time." Annie said and launched right into the first piece. Soon they were in the church sanctuary and performing the numbers.

Josie's first solo came up. She was a little hesitant at first, singing softer than the music required, but slowly gained confidence as Dona Nobis Pacem came out clearly. With the first one under her belt, Josie was able to belt out Angels From the Realms of Glory, just as it was meant to be sung, joyously. Love and joy radiated through her being as she sang The Gift of Jesus Christ. The rest of the service went by in a blur and ended quickly. They were back in the choir room, disrobing.

"Wasn't that an awesome service?" Roberta had come over to share in Josie's limelight, Josie thought. But, Roberta surprised her saying, "You did a great job on your solos, Josie! Keep up the good work!"

"Thanks, Roberta!" Josie said, her voice indicating her surprise at the other woman's attitude change.

"Oh, please! Call me 'Bobbie'. Everyone else does!" She smiled at Josie in a friendly manner for the first time. Josie returned the smile.

"Merry Christmas, Bobbie!" Josie said, still at a loss for words.

"See you at church next week!" Bobbie called as she turned and left.

"Huh. Miracles do happen on Christmas!" Josie said to herself. Then she also left to find her family. On the way upstairs and all through the hall, congregation members stopped her to congratulate her on her solos. She responded by saying, "Give God the glory!" and "Thanks! Merry Christmas!"

Josie had taken her coat straight to the choir room prior to church and left it on her chair. Having the entire choir do the same, Annie said, would leave more room on the coatrack for visitors to hang up their garments. The Colesons and Eleanor had prearranged to meet Josie and P.J. at home after church; so, Josie went out to the parking lot to find P.J. waiting for her in his car. He had had the foresight to go out to start it while he waited for her. She slid into the passenger seat and leaned over for a kiss before buckling up.

"You sang like an angel," P.J. told her. He put the car in gear and headed back to her house.

"You're just saying that because your my fiancée," she chided. "Honestly, now, how was it?"

"I told you, you were great. I even looked around to see what other people thought. They all had—what's the word—beatific smiles on their faces, like they were listening to a real angel!"

"Aw. You're so sweet," Josie said. "But, you don't have to make up things like that for me. I can take the truth."

They argued about it all the way home.

< * >

The Colesons left the Buchannon house shortly after Christmas Dinner. Even with all the fun they had, there were still presents under their own tree to open. The weather was sunny, but crisp as Mr. and Mrs. Coleson and the twins piled into their champagne colored Cadillac and headed home. P.J. and Josie promised to follow shortly. Eleanor wanted to give them their gifts before they left.

P.J. and Josie were seated on the carpet in front of the old-fashioned tree, minutes later, playing Santa. Josie would read the name on the gift tag and P.J. would place it in front of the person to whom it was intended.

"Open mine last, pussycat," Eleanor said as she rocked back and forth in the recliner. She still had on her red fitted Christmas dress and black pumps, while Josie had changed into wool slacks and a matching turtle neck sweater.

"Okay, Grams. Then you open yours first," Josie replied. P.J. nodded in agreement.

"Alright." Eleanor lifted the flat box from her lap and removed the card. She read the embossed lettering and smiled. Christmas wishes were just about the best greetings she had ever come across. Then she slid the satin ribbon off the corner of the box and lifted the gilded cover. Inside, nestled in white tissue paper, was a $200 gift card for Schwan's products, a Schwan's Catalog, and a handwritten note that said, "Grams, we know you love to cook, but sometimes it's nice to spend more time with you in the living room. Hope you enjoy this gift of time away from the kitchen. Love, Josie and P.J."

Eleanor smiled. She looked up and caught the expectant look on the kids' faces, and said, "You know, I was just thinking about ordering Schwan's service the other day when my friend, Nellie Pederson, was telling me how good the food is. She likes how easy and fast it is to prepare. She even likes her sales representative. You don't often find all that in one service. Thank you very much, Josie, P.J. I, too, will relish more time spent with you. We can play games or just visit. We won't always be living in the same house; so, what time we will have together will be that much more special. Now, open yours from me."

P.J. opened a rather large present, tearing into the wrapping with gusto. Inside the box, he discovered another box: a red toolbox, filled with hand tools. His eyes grew large as saucers.

"Wow!" He said, opening the toolbox and fingering the shiny hammer, pliers and socket wrench. "I can really take care of my car with these! That will save me lots of money on mechanic bills." He stood and gave Eleanor a hug. "Thanks! I really like them!"

"And, you can use them to help keep up the repairs on this house. Josie, open your gift, now, please."

Josie had a flat box much like Eleanor's. The gift wrap was in a different pattern, but the size was very similar. She opened the card, first, just as her grandmother had done. The card simply wished her many more happy Christmases with her soon-to-be husband. Josie tore off the wrapping and lifted the cover. As she lifted the tissue paper, she wondered which dress shop the gift card would be from. However, there was no card in the box. Instead there was a business size envelope taking up the entire interior. Josie lifted it out and opened it. She unfolded the multipage document and was stunned by what she read.

"Why, Grams, this is the deed to the house!" Josie looked from Eleanor to P.J. and back again, her mouth hanging open and eyebrows arched.

"Yes, dear," Eleanor said. She leaned forward in earnest. "With all the excitement of everything going on around here lately, I had noticed you hadn't had time to go house hunting. So, I hope you don't mind accepting the house as a combined Christmas and wedding present."

Chapter Eighteen
Confessions

Eleanor had explained to Josie and P.J. that she had arranged to move into the senior high rise that her friend, Nellie, lives in. She would be in good company and not have to worry about home repairs, mowing the lawn or paying property taxes, which of course, Josie and P.J. would take over. That suited them just fine and they both gave Eleanor a bear hug before leaving for New York City and more presents from the Colesons.

When they returned the next day, there was news from the FBI on how the investigation into Virginia's death was going. The call came in around 4 p.m. while Josie was at work.

"Good afternoon, Ms. Buchannon. I hope I didn't catch you at a bad time," Special Agent Freeman said over the line. Any time at work these days was precious; but, Josie knew this must be important or he wouldn't be calling her, so she took the call.

"If you have time to stop down to the station on your way home, I have some good news for you. I've already called your grandmother and she's agreed to meet us there, too."

"May I invite my fiancée, too?" Josie asked. She couldn't imagine going without P.J. She just hoped he didn't have to work late today.

"Certainly, that would be fine. I will see you in about an hour then. Goodbye."

Later, at the Lakewood Police Station, Josie and P.J. greeted Eleanor and went to the reception desk to announce their arrival. They were ushered into a conference room and waited for Special Agent Freeman to join them.

"I wonder what they found out," Josie said. P.J. and Eleanor nodded their agreement. Just then Special Agent Freeman breezed into the room and slid into a chair at the head of the table.

"I'm glad you could all make it," he said briskly. He always sounded like he was in a hurry to get to his next appointment. Today, his dark suit seemed a little wrinkled, like he'd had a particularly long day. "As I said on the phone, I have some good news. We have a break in the case."

"Well, what is it?" P.J. asked.

"We have interrogated Cassandra Coven, her guards and cellmates."

"Did she break?" P.J. was getting impatient; Josie could tell by the edge in his voice.

"No, she didn't. She's one tough cookie. But, her cellmates were all too eager to spill the beans. It seems she has had conjugal visits over the past six months or so."

"I thought you had to be married to have conjugal visits," Josie said. "Cass wasn't married. At least, not that we knew."

"Well, it seems that there's a lot about Coven we didn't know before," Freeman said. "Apparently she had been married before moving to Lakewood. Her ex-husband followed her here, and was rekindling their relationship. I ran him through Interpol and found out he's wanted for extortion and fraud in three states."

"What's he got to do with Virginia's death?" Eleanor asked.

"I'm just getting to that. I thought I'd connect some other dots along the way," Freeman said, mysteriously. Her husband's real name is Ramsey Lincoln; but, here, he goes by Raymond Potter. You may have heard of him, Mr. Coleson."

"Yes! He works at Lakewood Technologies in the research lab where I started out!" P.J. shouted and flew to his feet. "He must be the one who has been pulling all those pranks on me and causing all those accidents."

"We picked him up this morning for questioning. He's down in holding right now," Freeman said. He paused briefly for dramatic effect, apparently; then said, "He confessed to all those things; and, we have reason to believe he may have been the person who threw that rock into your sitting room window, Mrs. Buchannon. We just have to prove it."

Chapter Nineteen
To Catch a Cass & Other Fishy Characters

"How do you plan to prove Ray was the one who killed Mrs. Fieney?" P.J. asked, sitting down again. He crossed his arms and set his elbows on the table.

"We're gearing up for that right now," Freeman said. "We're going to put him in a lineup, then hook him up to a lie detector machine and interrogate him. We also plan to tell him we found a witness that saw him at your house the day of the incident. The neighbor had soon after left on a trip and only just got back, now, for Christmas. Then, if he's still reluctant to come clean, we will offer him a deal to cop to the lesser charge of vandalism and accidental death. See, we think he was just doing what Coven told him to. Every time he visited his ex-wife in prison, someone invariably overheard her telling him to do as she said as he was leaving. If he gives up his ex, he gets by with accidental death and vandalism instead of murder. He'll only spend 15 to 20 years in prison instead of life."

"I hope it works!" P.J. said vehemently. "Ray's been a pain in the butt ever since I started that job. I didn't know it was him, though. Maybe I should have because he was always such a smart ass at lunch and never shared any of his research findings with me. I just thought he was an arrogant researcher. There are some like that."

Josie reached out and touched P.J.'s arm to calm him down. He leaned back in his chair immediately.

"I hope justice is served and that these people can get the help they need to correct their errant thinking," Eleanor said.

"How soon will you know for sure?" Josie said.

"We'll have everything set up in about an hour. If you want to go grab some dinner and come back, you can watch from a nearby room," Freeman said.

"Through a two-way mirror like on TV?" P.J. said. "You bet!"

P.J. practically dragged Josie and Eleanor to the car and through a drive-through restaurant. He didn't want to miss any of the action; so, they took their burgers and fries back to the station and ate them in the same conference room they had been in earlier.

Exactly an hour after they had left the station for food, Special Agent Freeman returned to usher them to the viewing room from where they would watch the interrogation.

"I caution you to remain quiet during the entire proceedings. If you get noisy, I will have you escorted out of the building. You may sit in these cushioned chairs and don't move either. The two-way mirror isn't totally perfect. If Lincoln leaves his chair and comes near the mirror, he may be able to detect any movement on this side. Do I make myself clear?"

"Yes, sir!" they chorused and took their seats. Freeman left the room and shortly entered the next room. The three could see him through the mirror. He joined a polygraph technician who was already seated and working with his equipment.

"How's it going?" Freeman asked the other man.

"Ready to go, sir," the technician said.

Freeman went to the door to signal the guard. Presently, the guard returned with Ray Potter still in civilian clothes, but handcuffed. The technician told Potter to sit in the chair next to the lie detector machine. He did so and was strapped into it.

"This is the polygraph test for Raymond Potter, AKA Ramsey Lincoln," the technician said and included today's date. Apparently the officers were also recording the session. The technician launched into a series of innocent questions which Potter answered fluidly. Questions like: What is your name? Where are you from? Where do you work? Were you ever married? What is your ex-wife's name? Did you waive your right to having a lawyer present? He answered 'yes' to the last question.

Then came the trickier questions: Have you seen your ex-wife lately? Where did you meet with her? When was your last visit? What did the two of you talk about? Up until the last question, everything went smoothly. Potter was vague when answering the last question.

"Oh, you know, this, that, and the other thing," Potter sneered. He flipped his shaggy brown hair out of his face. "You know I only went there for one thing, and that wasn't to talk . . ." He raised his eyebrows and grinned exposing a sparkling smile.

"How about talking now?" Special Agent Freeman took over the questioning. "You were just in a lineup a couple hours ago. A neighbor of the Buchannons said they saw you hanging around the Buchannon house on the day Virginia Fieney was killed there. Someone threw a rock through the window which sliced off the old lady's head. What do you say about that?"

"I didn't go there to kill anyone," Potter said. "If I was there nobody saw me. That old biddy is lying." The needle on the polygraph machine took a leap.

"I didn't say it was a woman," Freeman said and watched Lincoln flush in anger. "Mr. Lincoln, do you do a lot of favors for your ex-wife?"

"Sometimes. Why?"

"Some of her cellmates have been telling tales on your conversations with her."

"What have they been saying? I bet it's all lies. They're just jealous I don't give them conjugal visits!"

"Actually, they've heard Cass reminding you to do favors for her every time you leave the prison. They've even heard what some of them are. Do you want to clarify what they are?"

"No."

"We've got enough evidence to lock you up for a long time, Mr. Lincoln. This lie detector told us enough to pin a murder rap on you."

"You can't make that stick."

"Are you willing to stake your life on it? As we speak, I've got an officer at the prison taking Cass's statement. Your ex-wife is rolling you over, buddy. With her telling the judge it was all your idea, that you wanted her to take you back and you'd do anything to get her to marry you again. You offered to harass her enemy, Josie Buchannon, you'll go to the electric chair for murdering Mrs. Fieney!"

"No! You can't do that to me! That lying bitch, Cass! No, it was her idea! She told me to scare the living daylights out of Josie and her grandmother."

"Give us the details, and we'll drop the murder charge down to manslaughter. You might even get early parole."

"Okay! The sun was glaring in my eyes. I didn't even see the old bag sitting near the window. And, who'd have thought the pane of glass would break in half like that? I thought it would just shatter. Anyone nearby would just get a few splinters in their hair, not get *killed*. That part wasn't my fault! You can't blame that on me! Hey, wait! I want my lawyer, now!"

"We have everything we need. Guard, get him out of here and let him call his lawyer, even though he waived one earlier." Freeman told the technician to carefully file the evidence with the D.A.'s office then left the room himself.

He entered the viewing room smiling. "Well, what did you think of that? He sang like a bird. Now all we have to do is turn on the same routine with Coven."

"Great job!" P.J. said, pumping the agent's hand.

"Thank you so much, Special Agent Freeman," Eleanor said. "Now I know Virginia will get justice."

"I don't think that method will work on Cass," Josie said quietly. She stared at Freeman. Everyone turned to look at her. They shook their heads like they couldn't believe their ears.

"Why would you say that?" Freeman asked. "You see how well it worked on Lincoln."

"You said it yourself. Cass was the mastermind behind all their scams, not Ray. I've known Cass longer than you. I know how cunning she can be. She's as smart as she is tough. The reason you didn't get anything out of her the first time is because she knows her rights, she knows how to work angles and how to find loop holes. She cheats whenever it suits her, and she's a fighter. She won't back down when you're trying to corner her."

"If you know her so well, what do you suggest?" Freeman asked, sitting in P.J.'s vacated chair.

"Let me go talk to her. I could say I came to forgive her, or some such stuff. She won't believe it, but it might be enough for her to let down her guard. She may brag about how much smarter she is than her ex-husband. She may even let it slip that she is the mastermind you think she is and take pride in her ideas. I'd have to wear a wire of course."

"Wouldn't that be dangerous?" Eleanor asked, placing her hand on Josie's shoulder.

"Not in the visitor's box," Freeman said, picking up the idea and running with it. "There's a bullet proof glass plate between the inmates and their visitors. The wire would have to be like a hearing aid though, because you'd be conversing with her by way of a telephone set. Yeah, that would work. We'll try that, and if it doesn't work, then we'll do it my way."

"You really didn't have an officer out at the prison during your interrogation of Ray did you?" P.J. asked. "That was just a ruse to get him to spill his guts, huh? All right! Real police action! Mislead the suspect enough to get him to confess. What a deal!"

"It's not all fame and glory, son," Freeman said. "Don't go running off to the police academy just because we got lucky tonight."

"Oh, don't worry," P.J. said. "I've got a wedding coming up. I can't afford to change careers at this time."

"You'd better not!" Josie and Eleanor said at the same time.

"Well, then. We'll call it a night," Freeman said, showing them the door. "Ms. Buchannon, please stop by after lunch tomorrow. We'll have the ear piece by then and an appointment for you to visit the prison. I'll even take you there myself. Goodnight."

< * >

"I can't believe I volunteered to do this!" Josie said over breakfast. Eleanor had whipped up some pancakes and sausages, saying Josie had to have a solid breakfast today, with the adventure she was going on this afternoon. "Sometimes my mouth moves before my brain has fully engaged."

"Josie, girl, you volunteered to do a brave deed that will help put away the right people for the right length of time. And, if there's any justice, Cass will get put in solitary confinement so that she has no more contact with troublemakers outside of prison," Eleanor said, having held her piece for far too long.

"And, I can't believe she was able to haunt us even after being put behind bars. I didn't know that kind of thing really existed. I thought that was just something writers dreamed up for movies and soap operas."

"One thing I've learned over the years, pussycat, is that life can be stranger than fiction, and you can't rely on fiction not being emulated by life, and vice versa. Now, drink your orange juice. You don't want to catch another cold."

Josie obeyed her grandmother, as usual, and pulled on her wool parka to go to work.

"Call me on the way back from the prison, so I will know you're all right," Eleanor said, and gave Josie a hug. "Stay warm, too! I'll be praying for you!" Josie waved and left by the back door for the garage.

At work Josie was a bundle of nerves. She finally broke down and called Vikki into the office.

"I've postponed my afternoon appointments," she told her best friend. "I can't tell you where I'm going or what I am going to do, except that it's 'classified'. And, I just had to tell someone. I know you can keep a secret."

"Of course, I'll keep your secret," Vikki said gently. "Will you be gone long?"

"I should be back tomorrow morning. Remember, don't tell a soul. If the staff asks where I went, just tell them I had an appointment outside of the office. They can make of that whatever they like. I'm sure most of them will think it's work-related. Everyone else will probably assume it's a doctor or dentist appointment. What they don't know won't hurt them, as the saying goes. I promise to take you to lunch tomorrow to fill you in on my mission."

"You make it sound so military. Oh, I know! You're going on an undercover assignment for the FBI! Just like you did last spring when you caught Cass in a sting!"

"Shhh!" Josie hissed. "Not another word. Right or wrong, just stop right there! You'll have to wait until tomorrow. Do you hear me?"

"Yes, Ma'am!" Vikki snapped to attention, turned on a dime and marched out of Josie's office.

Finally, 12 noon arrived; and, Josie fled the office. She couldn't wait to get this newest assignment in stupidity out of the way. She would be so glad when the New Year arrived; and, she could settle down to completing her wedding plans.

Once she arrived at the police station, the staff sergeant took her back to the briefing room where another technician fitted her with her hearing aid wire.

"With this baby, you don't have to do a thing. It has already been activated and won't need to be touched until you return and we remove it. Just remember to put the phone up to the ear with the wire in."

They both chuckled at the thought of her using the wrong ear. Luckily, the technician had asked her which ear she normally uses for phone calls.

Just then, Special Agent Freeman came into the room. He had on his winter overcoat and fedora, ready for the trip out to the prison.

"All set?" he asked one or both Josie and the technician. The tech nodded and left the room. Josie pulled her coat on and grabbed her purse, then, she too, nodded. They headed out to the agent's tan sedan in the parking lot. As the left the building, Freeman fingered his keychain and the engine started before they got there.

It was an hour trip on snow-covered roads to reach the women's state penitentiary. Freeman kept up a running chatter about the weather, the Giants going to the Super Bowl and Christmas cheer. Josie answered in monosyllables, trying to keep her mind on the pleasantries, and not on the impending encounter with her old nemesis. Finally, the gray, cement block building presented itself and they were stopped at the gate.

"Special Agent Freeman and Josephine Buchannon to visit inmate Cassandra Coven," Freeman said, flashing his badge.

"You're expected," the guard said, raising the gate. "Go on in. The warden is waiting for you."

Snow crunched underfoot as Josie and Special Agent Freeman walked from the parking lot to the steep steps of the main entry. They were happy to get inside the drab, but warm building. Just as the guard had said, Warden Warren Kennedy was waiting for them at the door.

"We don't often have civilians come in the capacity in which you are visiting us, Ms. Buchannon," the warden said, shaking her hand. "I am pleased to meet you and offer the services of my office, my staff, and my facility. If there's anything I can get for you, just name it."

"I'd ask for a bullet proof vest, but I'm given to understand that you have the highest safety rating in the entire New England area," Josie said.

"I'll wait in your office while Josie visits Cass," Freeman said. "Perhaps she could leave her coat and purse there as well?"

"Of course," the warden said. "Please follow me." They followed him; and, an armed guard followed them. Josie noted the prison guards wore the same brown and beige uniforms that the county sheriff's department did. The trio pattered a short distance to the main office, and the warden took out a set of keys to let them in. They went past the receiving desk to another locked door for which the warden also had a key. Inside, a huge metal desk took center stage. It was crowned with an overstuffed black leather executive chair and faced two teal covered barrel chairs. The warden gestured toward the barrel chairs, inviting the visitors to take a seat. Josie and Special Agent Freeman removed their bulky winter coats and hung them on the backs of the chairs before sitting in them.

Warden Kennedy took his chair and seated himself slowly, as a king would ascend his throne. Steepling his hands, with elbows on his desk, he leaned forward slightly and gazed at Josie.

"Keep in mind every second of your visit that you are in a state penitentiary," he advised. "This is not a vacation spot for rich people, nor is it a white collar crime resort. The inmates, while women, are convicts with rap sheets that include armed robbery, grand theft auto; and, like Ms. Coven, murder." He let that sink in before continuing. Josie nodded to show she understood; but, didn't dare speak. "Do not get yourself separated from your armed guard. You never know when a prison riot will break out. Do your best not to antagonize Ms. Coven or any other inmate.

"I understand you are fitted with a listening device, a wire that works like a hearing aid. Don't be surprised if Coven asks to see your wire. She will expect the old-fashioned kind, I'm sure. What you have is on the cutting edge of technology. And, if your techie didn't tell you, it works both ways. If you are in need of guidance during your visit, your man, Freeman, here will be talking in your ear. If you are in any kind of danger, your listening device will be your lifeline.

Are you ready?" Josie nodded again. "Captain Mike, here, will be your body guard. Go with him, now, and he will escort you to the visitors block."

Josie stood and turned toward the guard. "After you," she said, and followed him out the door. She could hear the warden locking the office door behind them. Then she focused on keeping up with the long-legged officer. He led her down a labyrinth of halls to a brightly lit reception area. There were a half dozen cubicles formed out of what Josie assumed to be bullet-proof Plexiglas. In each booth were two stools and a telephone receiver.

"Sit in this one," Captain Mike instructed. Josie sat and watched the wall on the other side of the Plexiglas. In just a minute, Cass appeared with her own uniformed guard. This one was female, Josie noticed, even though the officer had cropped her hair as short as a man's. Cass sat down in front of her; and, they both picked up their respective telephones.

"Orange goes well with your coloring," Josie said, reflecting her thoughts from the trial. Immediately, she blushed, feeling like a school kid.

"Thanks," Cass said, sarcastically. "So, what are you doing here? I'm not supposed to have any kind of contact with you, you know."

"Correction, please: You're not supposed to 'initiate contact' with me, my grandmother or P.J. You're not doing the initiating, I am." Hearing herself say the words 'I am' filled Josie with courage she didn't think was in her. And, maybe it had something to do with how irritating it was to have Cass act like she's in charge again. It just rubbed Josie the wrong way.

"So? I ask again, what are you here for?"

Taking a deep breath through her nostrils and releasing her tight lips, Josie said, "I came because I wanted you to know I forgive you for everything you've done to me and my family. I realize you've lived a hard life and when you finally thought you had something; and, someone—meaning me—seemed like they were going to take it from you, you felt threatened. Just like you said in the courtroom, you were just trying to protect what you worked so hard to get." Josie glanced down at her hand, her fingers tapping on the shelf in front of her. She was stalling, trying to think of her next line. She had thought she was ready for this inquisition. Now, in the heat of the moment, words failed her.

"If that's true, why should I be forgiven? If I was doing what I thought was right, and accidently killed Lew in the process, why am I being punished?" Cass emphasized the word accidently, as if to cover the truth.

Playing word games, again, huh, Cass? Josie thought. *Well, I'm not falling for that this time. I have to switch the topic.* "That was up to the court to decide. Speaking of court, I noticed you don't have your long fingernails anymore. I guess they would be considered 'lethal weapons' in here, huh?"

"Hah. Hah," Cass spat out, but conceded with a shoulder shrug. "No, they don't allow for much in here. We're lucky to get to comb our hair in the morning, and the guards watch us while we do. They confiscate the combs when we're done, so we don't carve them into weapons."

"Time to get to the point." Josie heard Freeman whisper in her ear. Startled, she cleared her throat.

"So, Cass! There's been scuttlebutt around town saying you've had conjugal visits here. You never mentioned you were married. I thought you were going to marry Lew." Josie blurted out.

"Now, you're going to pump me for information?" Cass asked warily. "What, you wearing a wire, or something?"

"Nope," Josie said confidently. She had been well-prepared for this. She didn't have to lie, either. She wasn't wearing a 'wire'. She was wearing a 'hearing aid', but wouldn't offer that information for the world.

"Prove it! Pull up your shirt!" Josie was ready for this, too, and complied, showing bare front and back. "Now, your pants—lose them!" Josie effectively mooned Cass, and grinned while doing so. "Okay. Cover that behind. I'm sick of looking at it already."

Josie pulled up her navy wool slacks and sat back down. She stared Cass in the eye and didn't back down.

"So, okay. You're not wearing a wire." Cass looked Josie up and down and then averted her eyes while she mulled over something.

"Alright, I'm not wired," Josie said. "What's this about a husband?"

"I guess it won't hurt you to know I was married. We pulled some scams in other states, then got into a fight and split up. I got one of those quickie divorces. No big deal." Cass flicked back her burnished blonde hair. Josie couldn't help but notice that it had grown out and her red roots were showing.

"What kind of scams, and what did you fight about?" Josie tried to keep her tone light, and not let her excitement show.

"My ex and I pulled some shady real estate deals and schmoozed elderly people into investing in fake companies. Some of the old biddies were even investing in Ray, if you know what I mean. Well, even crooks have standards. I say, if you're married, you're married. You don't sleep with other people. But, Ray, his greed exceeded his fidelity level. And, he pocketed the money he made pimping himself out. That's a double double-cross, in my book."

"So, Ray was a schemer, huh? He was the brains behind all your deals?" Josie could almost hear Special Agent Freeman breathing heavy with anticipation. Her palms were getting sweaty, though. She was praying she was right about Cass's ego. She'd want to take all the credit for having the smarts to pull off those jobs.

"No way. Ray's as stupid as a box of rocks. The only reason he made money as a gigolo is because he let his pecker do the thinking for him. And, his greed, like I said." Cass leaned in toward the glass divider and glared at Josie. *Oh, oh, she's on to me*, Josie thought, worried. But, she leaned in, too, like Cass was going to share a secret. Then hit pay dirt.

"Ray started losing money at the race track and at casinos. He got hooked on gambling. He spent more time doing that than doing his customers. So, he ran out of money. He remembered how good I was at coming up with schemes. And, of course, I had set aside a lot of what I made at Sanderson & Sons, so I had a nice little nest egg by the time he came running back to me. He begged me to take him back. So I said sure, if he did a couple of favors for me."

Josie could see Cass was ready to give the information they were all there for her to hear, so she chanced the invitation to continue. "What did you make him do for you, Cass?" she whispered encitingly.

"First he had to come here and pleasure me, nobody else. I decided to cheat on the conjugal visit application and put down just the date of our wedding, not our divorce. Besides, maybe my quickie divorce hadn't gone through. You never know about those cheap hustlers, right? Well, Ray let his pecker do his thinking for him again. Having a steady date would be a good thing for him too. Anyway, once we got that up and going, I asked him where he was living and where he was working. He said when he found out I was living and working in Lakewood, he figured that would be a smart move for him too. Before he even contacted me, he got a job at that research facility—what's it called—Lakewood Technologies. He said he was having fun picking on some new kid there, pulling pranks on him, and trying to get him in trouble with the boss. It was just like high school all over again for him."

"That was P.J., my fiancé, he was picking on." Josie said softly. Then to cover up she said, "That's who pulled all those pranks!"

"Yeah, well, I hear by the prison grapevine they put up cameras there, and Ray got caught."

"So? He'll just have to find someplace else to pull his pranks," Josie said, hoping to keep the conversation going. "Anyway, you said there were TWO things you asked him to do. What was the second, and did he do it?"

"Yes and no. That guy can sometimes get himself into a shitload of trouble just because he doesn't listen to details. I told him to hang around your house and scare you and your grandmother just for shits and giggles. I wanted to hear every detail about how you reacted to being stalked again." Cass's voice pitch dropped an octave. "I was looking for revenge, you know. And, have some fun while doing it, but not something serious that would point back at me. I told him to be careful. I told him not to get carried away; but, what did he do? He got carried away. He threw that rock through your window and killed that old lady! I know he said he didn't do it on purpose, that the sun was in his eyes and all that bullshit, but, man! He killed someone! I'll be lucky if they don't pin that on me too. I'll never see the light of day." Cass straightened up and looked over her shoulder to see how far away the guard was standing. She was three cubicles down, talking to someone else. So Cass leaned into the window again, and whispered into the mouthpiece, "Josie, I did NOT tell him to do that. You believe me, don't you?"

Just then, Special Agent Freeman rushed into the visiting area and tapped Josie on the shoulder. She turned to look at him.

"We have what we need. Let's go, now." Freeman was pulling on her arm. She turned back to Cass and said. "I believe you, but I think you still broke the conditions of your incarceration. See you! Or not." She hung up the receiver and stood to leave. Just then, two female guards had arrived. They took Cass by the arms. Josie saw Cass's face distort in rage, and her middle finger flipped up at Josie. Josie turned and fled the room with Freeman and Captain Mike.

They retraced their steps to the main office where the warden was waiting for them. He swiveled in his chair as they entered his office, waving a piece of paper.

"I just received this fax with a transcript of your conversation with Coven," he said, setting it on the desk. He reached into a side drawer and withdrew another piece of paper. He filled in the blanks on the form and pushed it toward Freeman. "I have all the proof I need to send Coven to solitary confinement for up to a year. I just need your signatures on this form as witnesses."

"That's because she sent Ray to make contact with us, isn't it?" Josie asked as she took the form from Freeman and put her own signature on it.

"Yes. Directly or indirectly initiating contact with your grandmother constituted a violation," Warden Kennedy said. Freeman agreed. "That's too bad too. She was proving to be a model prisoner. If she could have kept that up another seven years or so, she could have filed for parole."

shown to the front door by Captain Mike. The warden was held up with a telephone call.

The trip back to Lakewood was much more relaxed than the one to the prison. With the hard work behind them, even Josie let down her guard and chatted about her upcoming wedding with Special Agent Freeman. She noticed he really wasn't listening, but since he didn't stop her she just kept on letting off nervous energy. Then she remembered she had promised to call her grandmother to let her know she was on her way home safely. So, she pulled her cellphone out of her purse and dialed home.

When they arrived at the police station, P.J. was there to pick her up. He drove her home, listening to her excited chatter about the future. She was relieved she still had one.

"Oh, and, P.J., I promised Grams I'd give you both all the details of my mission over supper when we get home. I hope you don't mind, but I really only want to deliver this story only once. Then I want to put Cass out of my mind as solidly as she is going to be in solitary confinement." P.J. agreed and let her continue with her galloping discussion of their wedding plans. Mid-sentence, Josie's cellphone rings, and she answers it.

"Oh, hi, Special Agent Freeman," Josie glanced at P.J. to see if he was listening. "Yes, that would make sense. No, I have no issues with that. Yes, I will let my grandmother know—and my fiancé. Thank you very much! Good night!" Josie hung up and put her cellphone away before letting P.J. in on the message.

"Special Agent Freeman stated that since there was no evidence linking the mayor and his wife to Virginia's death or your accidents at work, he is going to visit them at their home in just a few minutes to let them know they have been cleared of all suspicion."

"I suppose that Cass's and Ray's stories corroborated enough to warrant closure," P.J. replied, and Josie nodded.

Over a pork chop and broccoli dinner that Eleanor had whipped up after hearing from her granddaughter, Josie relayed the conversation she had with Cass, how dreary the prison building was, and how terrified she had been to have to navigate with an armed escort the entire time.

"So Cass is in solitary confinement for how long?" P.J. asked.

"The warden said up to a year. He also said she had been a model prisoner up until she confessed she had sent Ray to harass us. Wait, I believe her exact word was 'stalk' us. That sounded horrible, but not as horrible as the results of his stalking." Josie stuffed another piece of pork chop in her mouth. She couldn't believe how flavorful it was. She particularly noticed how crispy Grams got the crust. Everything seemed to taste so much better now that Cass had been taken care of.

"Oh, I almost forgot something. Special Agent Freeman called as we were on our way here for supper. He said he was on his way over to the mayor's house to let them know the case is solved and that they are no longer suspects."

"Josie," P.J. was trying to get her attention. "I just remembered we haven't exchanged our Christmas gifts yet, just the two of us. I was wondering if we couldn't go out to dinner Sunday night, exchange gifts, then go to the New Year's Eve Ball at the community center. Would you like to do that with me?"

"It's New Year's Eve already?" Josie was astonished. Where had the time gone? Yes, New Year's Day is only a week after Christmas, and all the things she'd been through over the past twenty-four hours already seemed like a lifetime, but New Year's Eve, already? P.J. just nodded and waited expectantly.

"Go ahead, dear," Eleanor said. "I have plans to spend New Year's Eve at the senior apartments with Nellie and all our friends from card club. Nellie said I could stay at her place. You and P.J. deserve some time together after all you've been through."

"Oh, I agree, Grams. You don't have to twist my arm. I'm just going to have to get some sleep before then. And, maybe pull a Cass and take an afternoon off to go shopping. I don't have a ball gown."

"Well, to save your work reputation, how about using that gorgeous sapphire and rhinestone evening dress you wore when you went to California to open that new office with Garvey, Sloan & Associates last winter? I packed it away in blue tissue paper. It's in the cedar chest in my bedroom. I'll get it for you after supper, and you can try it on."

"Sounds like a fabulous plan, Grams," Josie said, and kissed Eleanor on the cheek. She turned to P.J., who was still waiting for an answer. "Yes, dear P.J., I would love to go out with you on Sunday night. As you heard, I do have a ball gown, so don't forget to rent a tux!"

Chapter Twenty
Wrap It Up

The office was crazy with excitement the next day. Everyone had heard on the radio how Josie had helped the FBI catch Cass again. She hadn't set more than a foot in the door when the entire staff clamored around her to hear the details of her mission.

"Let's go into the conference room, and I'll tell you all about it—just once. Give me five minutes to settle in first. Vikki, make your usual arrangements so you can be there too." With that, she headed back to her office, and the staff followed suit. Before she even set her briefcase down, Josie was on the intercom making an announcement, "Be sure to bring your reports and notebooks with you. This will be our staff meeting for the week. Thank you!" Then she set her briefcase on the desk and hung up her parka. She slumped into her chair and felt deep in her bones how good it was to be back to work. Maybe today would be the day she could work uninterrupted and not have to postpone any appointments. Even Special Agent Freeman said she could come in at her leisure to debrief.

Josie opened her briefcase and took out her laptop. She booted it up and prepared for the staff meeting by printing out the handouts she had worked up after P.J. had left the night before. She had been too keyed up to get any sleep, so she opted to do something more constructive than stare at the shadowy ceiling of her bedroom. Copies and laptop in hand, she headed to the conference room.

"Good morning, again! I see you must have rushed right in here since you all beat me." She set her laptop at the head of the conference table and gave the stack of copies to Vikki to distribute. Then she sat down in her executive chair to start the meeting.

"First, let me say, 'Don't try this at home!'" Everyone chuckled at that. Then she launched into a reenactment of her visit to the state penitentiary. Since Cass was already being disciplined for her breach of sentencing guidelines, there was no harm in sharing the information with her staff. When she finished her story, everyone was exclaiming how brave she had been.

"Oh, my! Weren't you scared?" Vikki asked.

"Do you know Tae Kwon Do? Could you have defended yourself if a riot had broken out?" Jessica wanted to know.

"I would have kicked some inmate-butt, if I were you!" Hildy exclaimed.

"I wonder how big a budget they need to run a place like that. Do they have government grants, or how do they pay their bills?" Nathan scratched his head.

"There was an armed guard at my side the entire time. There was no need for concern," Josie said. "And, I wasn't there to discuss their budget, so I don't know the answer to that question. However, you could probably Google it.

"Now, it's time to settle back to the everyday chore of running an advertising business. I need to hear your weekly reports. What happened this past week when I was out so much? What are we going to do going into the New Year to counteract any slump in business? Let's hear from Nathan first, so we have a basis on which to build our projections."

"The bottom line, as you can see by this graph," Nathan stood and pointed to the projection screen, "did dip some last week. I predict, with the holidays and Josie's postponements, the income will dip a bit again this week. But entering the New Year, if everything is back on track, we can recoup the losses within the first month."

Everyone else's reports went smoothly, indicating that with Josie gone a couple of days, all the staff members had caught up on their work and were ready to help her pursue new clients. Josie was impressed with their enthusiasm and positive attitudes. She thanked them for it and for their reports.

"That about wraps it up," Josie said, standing. "Let's go ahead and start recuperating!"

The busy workweek gave way to the weekend. Josie felt confident that the firm was back on track, so she sent her staff home a half hour early on Friday, saying if any of them needed to take care of any last minute plans for celebrating the New Year, this was the time to do it.

"Just come back Tuesday ready to work. No three-day hangovers, please," she advised. Then she packed up her laptop, donned her winter coat and left early as well. *Whoosh,* she let out a gust of air. "I had better not get used to this or that bottom line will never come up!" she said to herself.

Instead of going out Friday night, P.J. and Josie had decided to have a quiet dinner at his apartment. After work Josie had stopped by the meat market on the way over to his place. She picked up a couple of fine looking rib eye steaks and told the butcher to wrap them up. She also selected a pound of Colby Jack cheese for hors d'heurves. As she got out of her car in the apartment parking lot, P.J. pulled into the space next to her. He hopped out of the car and took the grocery bag from her.

"I hope you teach our children to be as courteous and helpful as you are," Josie said and gave him their usual greeting kiss.

"And, I hope they all look as gorgeous as you!" P.J. countered. "Even after the week you've had. Here is it Friday, after work, and you still look breathtaking!"

"Your breath has been taken by this cold weather!" Josie declared. They laughed and started toward the door.

"So, what are you cooking me for supper, tonight, my darling fiancée?" P.J. asked, trying to peak into the bag.

"I was hungry for steak, so I stopped at that butcher shop we like so well and found a couple of thick rib eye. I hope that's okay with you, my dear, handsome future husband." He reached down and nuzzled Josie's nose in answer. She giggled. P.J. then whipped out his apartment key and let them in.

They worked together to get supper on the table quickly, and sat down and enjoyed it slowly. They talked about the weather, the great-tasting steak, the impending New Year's Eve Ball, and everything and anything except the problems they had encountered over the past few months. They were determined, with unspoken agreement, to avoid distasteful subjects for the entire weekend. After supper, they worked in tandem again, to get the dishes in the dishwasher and to have a cozy evening in front of the television. Josie left about 11 o'clock, promising P.J. she would sleep in the next morning.

After a long, sweet kiss in the hall, P.J. said, "Remember, don't even set your alarm tonight. You have nothing to get up for except to get ready for our New Year's Eve date!" Josie just threw a wave and a mischievous grin at him and left.

The sun was up before Josie was the next morning. She kept her word and slept in. She stretched and lounged under the covers for a few more minutes before throwing back the blankets and sitting up to greet the day.

"Hello., sunshine!" Josie said, and started humming the tune to The Happiest Girl in the Whole U.S.A. as she pulled on her white chenille bathrobe and slippers. She was full-out singing, "Thank you, Lord, for making him for me . . ." as she made her way downstairs to breakfast.

"So, it's a 'skippety-doo-dah day', is it?" Eleanor greeted Josie, and they exchanged pecks on the cheek. Josie practically floated into her chair while Eleanor finished up at the stove.

"It certainly is. And, tomorrow night is going to be a fabulous celebration of life!"

"In the meantime though, you are going to eat brunch with me, right?" Eleanor set the platter of French toast on the table and went to the refrigerator for fruit cups.

"Sure, Grams, anything you want, and after brunch, I am going to make a couple more phone calls to people I want in the wedding. Last night P.J. and I decided on a vocalist and an organist. No, shush. Don't ask, yet. I want to see if they say, 'Yes', before I tell you. I will say this; you will be surprised at one of them!" Eleanor sat down at the table, bowed her head and led Josie in the dinner prayer. Then they feasted.

Later Eleanor was in the hall and accidently overhead one of Josie's wedding calls.

"Good morning, Bobbie! How are you today?" Josie paused to hear the other woman's answer. "I know this is kind of out of the blue and all, but P.J. and I would love to have you sing for our wedding. Please say, yes!" Another pause. "Great! I just got off the phone with Annie. She said she would play organ for us and accompany you. Let's do lunch on Tuesday, the three of us, and I'll tell you the songs I want you to sing, okay? Wonderful! See you then!"

When Josie hung up, Eleanor moved away from the door, smiling.

After doing not much of anything for the next 24 hours, Josie took a hot bubble bath and started primping for her date with P.J. He said he would pick her up around 6 o'clock, and he's never been known to be late. So Josie made sure she was dressed and ready to go by quarter to six. At that time she drifted downstairs and asked her grandmother to help her with her necklace. It was a sapphire heart with one small cubic zirconia in the center. It was a gift from Grams last Christmas, and Josie hoped it would inspire P.J. to give her a ruby one like it for Valentine's Day.

"Wouldn't you rather go without a necklace, dear, just in case P.J. is giving you one tonight?" Eleanor asked. "That way your neck will be bare, and give him opportunity to put the new one on you."

"That would be much more romantic than my struggling to take this one off first, wouldn't it?" Josie asked in agreement. "Okay, I'll leave this one home."

Just then, the doorbell rang. Eleanor strode to the door and let P.J. in.

"You're five minutes early," Eleanor greeted him. "You must be anxious to get this date underway."

"Yes, Ma'am," He replied, adjusting his bow tie.

"P.J., how many times have I told you to just walk in," Eleanor scolded him. "You're going to be family soon. Please don't stand on ceremony any longer."

"Yes, Grams!" He said with a grin.

"That's more like it! Now, turn around so I can see you. Don't you look dapper! I can just imagine you in your wedding tuxedo! Josie, P.J.'s here!" she called. Both their eyes went to the door of the living room from where Josie emerged sparkling like a rare gem. She smiled and glided over to greet P.J. They kissed. Eleanor cleared her throat to remind them she was still there. They broke apart, and Josie turned to give her grandmother a goodbye hug.

"Well, you're not sixteen anymore, so I suppose giving you a curfew is out of the question," Eleanor hugged her back. "Be sure to take your wool cape. Your parka just won't do, and it's too cold out there to go without something even if P.J. has thoroughly warmed up his car." They waved at her as Josie took her cape from the entry closet. P.J. helped her put it on and then held the door for her. Josie gave Grams another quick kiss on the cheek and headed out into the night.

"Your eyes are sparkling like the stars," P.J. told Josie as he drove to the Fireside Restaurant where he had made reservations. "That dress is very pretty. Where did your grandmother say you had worn it before? California?" It took the rest of the drive for Josie to explain the Cinderella trip she took as the newest member of the Garvey, Sloan & Associates Advertising Firm where his mother worked.

"Didn't you mom ever tell you about it?"

"If she did, I was too busy breaking up with Priscilla to pay attention," P.J. admitted. "Sorry about that. I promise that from this day forward I will pay close attention to everything you say and do. Now let's go in and eat."

The maître de showed them to a private table in a back corner. It was dimly lit by a single candle setting in the center of the table. Josie glided into the rounded corner booth and made room for P.J. beside her. He discreetly tipped the maître de and sat beside her.

"This is very elegant, P.J. Thank you!" She whispered in his ear.

"Nothing is too extravagant for my bride-to-be on our first New Year's Eve together."

The waiter interrupted them, gave them menus and the evening's specials, then took their drink order. P.J. ordered an O'Doul's, and Josie ordered water with lemon. When they were alone, again, P.J. pulled a long, thin box from the inside pocket of his tuxedo coat. He handed it to Josie.

"Merry Christmas!" he said. "I hope you like it." Josie pulled the bow off the top of the box and lifted the lid. She gasped in surprise and joy.

"Oh, P.J.! It's beautiful!" Josie gazed fondly at the sapphire and diamond necklace cradled in sky blue satin. "Oh, you have to help me put it on!" *Oh, Grams! I'm going to get you! You knew about, this didn't' you!* Josie thought in a teasing manner. P.J. put the delicate strand around Josie's neck and latched it. Then he handed her a broad table knife to use as a mirror.

"Your grandmother let me see the dress the other night while you were in the bathroom. She told me how romantic it would be if I bought you a necklace to match and helped you put it on." He kissed Josie's neck, delicately tracing the white gold chain of the gift.

"She was right, this is so romantic!" She held P.J.'s face between her hands and gave him a fat smooch. "Thank you so much!" Then she pulled out her dainty evening bag, which didn't look like it could hold more than a Kleenex. She opened it and slid her small hand inside, only to draw it out almost immediately. She took P.J.'s left hand in hers and brought up a man's sapphire and diamond ring with a white gold setting.

"The 'in thing' now is men's engagement rings," Josie said, slipping the ring on his finger. "P.J., I've said yes to your marriage proposal, please say yes to mine. Will you wear this ring as a symbol of my love and our commitment to get married?"

P.J. held out his hand and inspected the ring. "Yes, of course I will. You did an excellent job picking it out. This is great!" He leaned down and kissed Josie, his arms tightened around her, and she leaned into the kiss. The waiter returned with their beverages, interrupting them. He left the drinks on the table and excused himself.

"P.J., tell me how you picked out this necklace," Josie asked.

"I just went into the jewelry store your grandmother suggested. They only had one diamond and sapphire necklace on hand. I just told the jeweler to wrap it up!"